Secrets...hopes...dreams...

Welcome to

*Silver *Spires

where

School Friends

are

forever!

Collect the *School Friends* series:

Rivalry
at
*Silver
*Spires

Ann Bryant

USBORNE

With grateful thanks to
Kate Steel, Neil Rawlinson, Claire Thompson
and Chloe Swan, for their invaluable help

First published in the UK in 2008 by Usborne Publishing Ltd.,
Usborne House, 83-85 Saffron Hill, London EC1N 8RT, England.
www.usborne.com

Series cover design by Sally Griffin
Cover illustration by Suzanne Sales/New Division

The name Usborne and the devices ♀ 🎈 are Trade Marks of
Usborne Publishing Ltd.

A CIP catalogue record for this book is available from the British Library.

First published in America in 2013 AE.
PB ISBN 9780794531515   ALB ISBN 9781601303004
JFMAMJJ SOND/12   01565/3
Printed in Dongguan, Guangdong, China.

Chapter One

I love this moment of walking through to the school pool from the changing room. My whole body comes alive, even more than it does on the athletics field. Maybe it's something about the smell, or the steamy atmosphere, or the beautiful pale green water that reminds me of the sea back home in Thailand. Whatever it is, I love it. I always find my footsteps speeding up, because I'm so desperate to get into the water and swim and swim. But this time Jess's hand on my arm stopped me in my tracks.

"Grace, look!" she said in her dreamy voice. Her eyes were on the far window, which goes all the way from the floor to the ceiling. "Look at that sun shining in. Isn't it beautiful? The water looks like liquid gold up at the deep end, doesn't it?"

I smiled at my best friend. "I bet you'll do a painting of that later, won't you?"

But she didn't answer because she was lost in a little Jess-daydream. By now there were quite a few people in the pool. I hadn't seen anyone diving in yet, though, so I decided not to do that either. It might have seemed like I was showing off and that was the last thing I wanted anyone to think.

Mrs. Mellor, our wonderful PE teacher, was hurrying people out of the changing room while the lifeguard sat on high and watched over us all. I went down the steps and felt the cold water rising up around me, and although it made me shiver, it was a shiver I loved. It took me straight back to swimming in the sea in Thailand over the Christmas break. This is the beginning of spring at Silver Spires, which is the most perfect boarding school in the world, and here I am about to start our very first swimming lesson, because we didn't have any actual scheduled swimming before Christmas. I should be totally happy, but there's just a small chunk of happiness missing because I can't help feeling a little homesick. My mom and dad and my big sister seem so far away when I'm at school. I know I've got my amazing group of friends, including my very best friend, Jess, and I also know I'll soon be back in boarding-school mode, but it's only the first year of boarding for all us sixth graders so we're still getting used to it.

"Oh no! This is torture!" came good old Georgie's voice. I glanced over to see her hunched up at the top of the steps.

"The quicker you get in, the quicker the torture – as you call it – will be over!" said Mrs. Mellor firmly. She clapped her hands. "Chop-chop, everyone! Five minutes' free swimming to get used to the water and then we'll start the lesson." She went over to help someone tighten their goggles a bit, then turned back around. "Georgie Henderson, your challenge is never to be the last one in the pool."

Georgie didn't answer, just hunched her shoulders even more and folded her arms, while her best friend Mia jigged up and down in the pool in front of her. "You'll get used to it really quickly, honestly!" I heard her say, as I set off to the deep end, doing front crawl.

I was concentrating hard on making my body as narrow and straight as possible, bringing my arms right over my head and cutting through the water with the side of my hand, while keeping my legs and feet strong. My parents wanted me to have swimming coaching during the break but in the end I only had three sessions because our wonderful Christmas celebrations went on for so long this year, with lots of visitors and outings. It was hard leaving those hot sunny days of fun behind and coming back to the winter chill at school.

When I got to the deep end I stopped and looked around. If I half closed my eyes the surface of the pool looked like pale green silk with lots of brightly colored balls floating all over it. We have to wear caps for swimming and each boarding house here at Silver Spires has its own color. My five close friends and I are in one of the sixth grade dormitories in Hazeldean House and we've all got purple hats. The girls from Willowhaven wear green hats, Beech House wear blue, Forest Ash, red, Elmhurst, white and Oakley, yellow. I love it that girls from all the different houses are mixed together completely randomly for things like sports and music and art. Then for math, science and English classes we're in first, second and third sets.

Mrs. Mellor blew her whistle to announce that we only had another two minutes of free swimming and I suddenly realized I was starting to shiver because I'd been still for a while and wasn't fully warmed up. I set off back to the shallow end doing the fastest crawl I could manage and then turned around and headed straight back to the deep end, trying to do the proper breathing on every third stroke, but not managing it very well because breathing for the crawl stroke is my biggest weakness. I'd almost completed the second length when, through the blur of the water, I noticed a blue hat coming up on my left. Someone from Beech House was swimming really fast. We touched the side at exactly the same time and when she turned to face me, I realized it was a girl named Felissia Streeter. I smiled at her, but all I got back was a cold stare and I felt horrible shivers pushing through the nice warmth I'd gathered during my hard swim. I didn't know what that look was about and I don't like it when I don't understand things.

Mrs. Mellor's whistle made me jump and I was glad that I had to concentrate on listening to instructions about lining up at the deep end because it took my mind off Felissia's horrible look. The rest of the lesson was great fun because Mrs. Mellor always makes everyone feel so confident, and we tried all the different strokes, even butterfly, which I'm hopeless at. I loved all the other strokes and didn't want the swimming lesson to end.

"That was great fun," said Jess, in the changing room afterwards.

"I wasn't very good," said Georgie.

"Neither was I," added Naomi. "I just didn't seem to ever get warmed up."

"I thought you were really good," said Katy, who's Naomi's best friend. She grinned at me as she rubbed her hair with a towel. "But we knew you'd easily be the best of our group, Grace."

Jess shuffled closer to me on the bench. "We're so lucky having you in our house," she said.

"And we've got Katy too," I quickly pointed out, because Katy's a strong swimmer.

"Are you two joining the swim team?" Mia asked.

We weren't sure whether just anyone could join the team, because the team isn't a fun thing like a club. It's much more serious. So Katy went to ask Mrs. Mellor. She came back with the answer that if you want to do the swimming competition you *have* to join the team, but anyone's allowed to sign up for it and see how they do. "But *you've* definitely got to join, Grace!" she added. "You're the best!"

"With some luck you can enter *all* the races, Grace, and the rest of us can just cheer you on. Then Hazeldean will be the winning house! Yay!" Georgie was pulling her sweatshirt over her head so we could only just make out what she was saying, but the others all laughed, apart from Jess. She probably guessed I'd be feeling anxious about all this praise because I'd already told her I didn't feel as confident about swimming as I did about other sports.

"There are some really good swimmers in the other houses," I said quietly, and I couldn't help glancing around for Felissia. I spotted her in front of the mirror scooping her hair up into a ponytail.

"Felissia Streeter's good, isn't she?" said Mia, who must have followed my eyes.

I nodded and suddenly felt tempted to tell the others about Felissia's look, but I didn't because it would have sounded like such a silly little thing. And as soon as I'd had that thought, I realized that actually, that's exactly what it was – a silly little thing – and I told myself to stop worrying and forget about it.

But just before bedtime it popped back into my head again. We were up in our dormitory admiring each other's bulletin boards. Jess's was covered with photos she'd taken during the holidays, but they weren't the usual kind of photos of people or scenes; they were all of different sorts of trees, like close-ups of gnarled old bark, or thin bare trees silhouetted against the white sky. She's got such a big imagination, Jess has, and I really love the way she looks at the world. We're so different from each other and we both think that's the very thing that makes us best friends.

Katy's board was artistic too, but in a different way. Hers was covered with fashion pictures, because that's Katy's biggest passion. Naomi's had photos of elephants and deer roaming across stretches of scrubland with barely anything growing. That's because she comes from Ghana in Africa. In fact, it's easy to forget that Naomi is actually a real live African princess. She's so modest and never boasts about it at all. Her family lives here now but she still thinks of herself as Ghanaian and I knew she'd been back to Ghana over the holidays because she mentioned a charity that she's working for called Just Water, which helps the people of Ghana to have access to clean water. Naomi and I had also talked together about how far from home we both felt, and how winters are here compared to our own countries. We're not the only ones who come from far away though. There are girls from all five continents at Silver Spires.

Georgie was admiring the way Mia had made photos of her pets and her family into a collage.

"When I tried to do that with my pics, I chopped off half the heads!" she said, frowning. "And what's the point of having the best actors in the world right over your bed if they're headless?"

"Do you want me to rearrange them a bit for you?" asked Mia.

But Georgie was standing in front of my bed by then, hands on hips, pretending to be disapproving. "Don't say we've got to look at a bunch of athletes again, Grace! Is that all you think about – sports?"

"You're only jealous, like the rest of us, Georgie!" said Jess.

Georgie's eyes shifted from my board to me. "Yes, I *am* jealous! Why can't I look like Grace? I'd love to be slim and fit. I wish I could run like a deer and jump like a…like a…kangaroo."

I laughed. "I hope I don't look like a kangaroo when I'm jumping!"

Georgie ignored me. "And I'm very jealous of your fantastic swimming too!"

Naomi put her arm around me. "Yes, we've definitely got the best swimmer in sixth grade in our house!"

Katie rubbed her hands and grinned like a mischievous little girl. "I bet the other houses are green with envy!"

"Don't say that," I quickly told them, feeling myself getting anxious again. "I'm not all that good at swimming, you know. There are lots of sixth graders who are better than me. I'll have to train like crazy."

"Nonsense!" said Katy. "You're just as great at swimming as you are at every other sport!"

All this praise was exactly what I'd been dreading. That's why I'd felt tense every time I'd thought about the swimming competition during Christmas. It was due to take place before spring break, and with all the training I wanted to do, that didn't seem far enough away. It's a horrible pressure when people expect you to do well at something, and it's not only my friends, but my parents and the teachers here too. You see, I came to Silver Spires on a sports scholarship, which means that my fees for the school have been paid because the school thinks I'm going to do really well at sports, so that when we have inter-school competitions I'll win and that will make other schools admire Silver Spires. I don't feel so much pressure when it comes to other sports like volleyball, because I'm confident about them. But swimming's different. I'm not so good at swimming.

I had to make the others realize. "No, honestly, I'm not just saying it. At home my sports coach says that swimming is my weakest thing, so I've made a resolution to train hard. Only, it might not make much difference, you know."

"You can only do your best, can't you?" said Naomi, who's the wise one of the group. "And remember you'll have swim team as well."

I looked around hopefully. "I'm not going to be the only one doing swim team, am I?"

"Well, don't look at me!" Naomi laughed. "I'm allergic to cold water."

"Me too," said Mia, wrinkling her nose.

"The trouble is, it clashes with fashion club," said Katy, "because it's on Wednesdays. Oh, by the way, Mrs. Mellor said they're not meeting for swim team this coming Wednesday though, because she's away."

Then Jess surprised me. "I might come," she said, her eyes looking dreamy as they so often did. "I enjoyed floating on my back and staring at the ceiling in the lesson today. It's got an incredible pattern on it, you know, like an optical illusion."

I had to smile. "You're such an artist, Jess! Imagine noticing the swimming pool ceiling!"

"Okay, that's enough swimming talk for one day!" Georgie suddenly announced. "I'm off to the computer room."

Everyone decided to check their e-mails then, so we all trooped down two flights of stairs to the computer room.

"Good, we're the only ones here!" said Katy. "One computer each."

"We've only got a few minutes before we have to get ready for bed," said Mia, who gets even more anxious than me about rules and regulations. I don't know about Mia, but for me I think it's because my parents brought me up pretty strictly and always expect me to respect my elders.

"Yay! Loads of people online!" said Georgie, who's really into the Silver Spires chat room at the moment.

The rest of us were quickly checking our e-mails. I had a long one from my mom, and although it was nice to hear from her it made me feel a little homesick too. Out of the corner of my eye I could see that Mia had finished on her computer and was leaning on Georgie, watching her screen.

I'd almost finished reading Mom's e-mail when I suddenly heard a gasp from Mia.

"What?" I heard Katy ask.

There was no reply and I glanced around to see that Mia's eyes were wide and worried.

"What are you looking at?" Naomi wanted to

16

know, and a few seconds later we were all bunched around trying to read the message on Georgie's screen.

Someone with the username *Torpedo Gal* had written, *Shame about the big show-off who just has to be best at everything she ever does, including swimming.*

"That's not very nice. Who's written that?" asked Mia.

Georgie didn't answer at first, just started typing back. *What big show-off?*

We all watched the screen as the message came back. *You should know. You'd better warn her that we don't like show-offs and it's about time she gave someone else a chance to win.*

"So who *is* *Torpedo Gal*?" asked Naomi.

"I don't have a clue," said Georgie, in a surprisingly quiet voice. "I've got so many people on my contact list I don't know who I'm talking to half the time." Her voice faltered. "But whoever it is knows who *I* am."

A horrible prickly feeling was creeping up my spine.

"But who's she talking *about*?" asked Katy.

There was a small silence, and then everyone must have clicked that it could only be me. Georgie turned around and gave me a kind of apologetic smile, at the same time as Jess's arm went around my shoulder, and the prickly feeling spread right up to the backs of my eyes.

Chapter Two

No matter how much my friends kept telling me to forget about the stupid chat room, I simply couldn't forget it. I kept on remembering the look that Felissia had given me in the pool and I just knew that she was the person who'd sent those nasty messages, and that it was obviously me she was talking about. I was so upset that if it hadn't been for Jess and the others persuading me, I probably would never have signed up for swim team, and then I wouldn't have been able to take part in the competition. To make matters worse it turned out that swim team clashed with fashion *and* art club, so Jess wouldn't be able to come with me after all. Felissia's name wasn't on the list yet, thank goodness, but there was still plenty of time.

For days since my horrible shock in the computer room, the six of us had kept coming back to the same conversation about those chat-room messages time and time again. Well, to tell the truth, *I* was usually the one who kept coming back to it. I just wished there was a way of finding out who had written the messages and whether or not she definitely had been talking about me. I'd been planning on doing some training during the weekend, but in the end I hadn't gone to the pool at all because I couldn't bear to think that there might be someone there watching me and thinking I'm a show-off, without me knowing about it.

By Thursday I'd even gotten myself worked up about the swimming lesson the next day. But it was Jess who brought up the subject when we were walking across to afternoon classes.

"Couldn't you just go around asking people what their usernames are, Georgie?"

"But I've got such a massive contact list, like I said," Georgie answered.

"Like the whole sixth grade," said Mia, rolling her eyes.

"Plus people change their usernames all the time," Georgie went on. "Like if the weather suddenly got cold they might have the username *Isn't it cold?*"

I sighed a deep sigh and spoke quietly because I didn't seem to have much energy. "I can't bear to be called a show-off."

"You're totally not a show-off!" said Jess, raising her voice and looking cross. "That's why I don't see how that message can have been about you!"

"Anyway, whoever it was is just jealous," said Mia firmly.

Every single one of my friends had said these things lots of times already, but what Katy said next, in a low voice, hadn't actually been said by anyone, not even me.

"I bet it's Felissia Streeter."

"I was wondering about her too," admitted Mia, "but I didn't dare say it."

I swallowed.

"It's true that she hates it when you beat her in athletics," said Georgie, "like that time she pretended she'd sprained a muscle when you won the two hundred meters."

That was exactly the thought I'd been having myself. You see, I once heard Felissia boasting to her friends that she'd gotten a sports scholarship to Silver Spires, which means that her parents pay less. She said that the main reason she got the scholarship was because she was easily the best swimmer at her school, and also because she'd once swum in the under-elevens team for her state. So I knew that swimming meant a lot to Felissia and I guessed she probably wanted to be the best. From what I'd seen in the lesson last week, I thought she probably was the best too.

"Maybe she got fed up with always coming second to Grace in athletics and things," said Katy.

Mia nodded, but I could tell she felt a little nervous. "And now she wants to be the very best at swimming, because that's kind of...her thing."

"Hang on a sec," said Naomi. "We've got no proof who *Torpedo Gal* is, or even that she's talking about Grace. I think you should just forget about it, Grace, and carry on as normal. Whoever it is, they haven't been back online since, so maybe that's the last Georgie will hear from them."

"Yes, and whenever you want to start training, you should go right ahead!" said Jess. "I might not be able to join the team, but I can always come to training with you, Grace, and do some floating!"

I felt lucky to have all my friends caring so

much about me. And I knew Naomi was right – it would be stupid to let some anonymous message worry me.

"Okay, quick change, girls! Chop-chop! No messing around!" said Mrs. Mellor, smiling at everyone. "Last week I was gentle with you. This week I want action! First one in the pool gets three credits! And leave your towels in the changing room, please." Then she went through to the pool herself and the student teacher, Miss Snow, stayed with us. I moved to the far end of the bench away from the others, as we were all a little squashed, and there was a crazy scramble to get changed quickly because credits count toward the House Cup. "Mrs. Mellor says if anyone leaves clothes on the floor, the credits don't count, I'm afraid, girls," said Miss Snow.

I got excited as I stuffed my clothes deep into my swimming bag, because I've always been quick at changing and guessed I was in with a good chance of being first. I don't usually mind not wrapping myself in my towel to go through to the pool, but right now I was wishing it was allowed. It would be good to hide under it. I wouldn't feel on view so much.

"See you in the pool!" I called to Naomi and Katy

as I shot out of the changing room.

It was weird seeing the pool completely empty because even when I'd done free swimming there had always been at least one other person there. I didn't have time to think about that now, though. All I had to do was get straight in and I'd have three credits, just like that. My feet hardly touched the steps at all as I slithered in.

"Well done, Grace!" said Mrs. Mellor, as a chilly gasp surged through my body. Then immediately afterwards I heard a splash and saw that Katy and a girl named Jemma had gotten in at exactly the same time. "Better luck next time, Katy and Jemma. Grace just beat you. But I'll give you one credit each for being so close behind. Get yourselves warmed up while the others are coming through, girls."

I'd already started swimming to get warm, but I turned to give Katy a thumbs up and that's when I saw Felissia standing on the edge, dipping her toe in the water.

"Wow! That's got to be a designer suit she's wearing," said Katy quietly, swimming alongside me on her back.

I wanted to forget about Felissia, so I just said "Mmm," then turned over and did front crawl up to the other end, hearing the laughter and dramatic screeches of more and more girls getting in the pool. By the time my hand touched the far wall I felt completely warm and realized I wasn't half so nervous any more. There's something about being held up by water that calms my body, and for a little while, as I swam up and down without looking around, I felt completely happy. I told myself to try not to look at Felissia at all, all the way through the lesson, and then everything would be fine. It was getting noisier and noisier but Mrs. Mellor didn't seem to mind. She was watching everyone carefully though, and I knew she'd be assessing us all.

Once everyone was warmed up, Mrs. Mellor split us into three groups of six and asked the first group – which included me, but unfortunately Felissia too – to come up to the deep end. She told all the others to go with Miss Snow to the shallow end to work on breaststroke leg kicks. All my friends were with Miss Snow.

"I don't usually teach techniques for races in normal swimming lessons," Mrs. Mellor began, crouching down at the side and looking at us, "but you six have all signed up for swim team so I want to get started on practicing turns." My spirits sank a little now I knew that Felissia was definitely going to be in the swim team. "Line yourselves up ready to go across the width of the pool," Mrs. Mellor said, "and on my whistle, starting with Felissia, swim front crawl to the other side, then turn around and swim straight back. When you've each had a turn we'll talk about the way you turned around, so watch each other carefully."

Felissia set off smoothly and when she got to the other side she did a flip turn, which is the correct way to turn around in swimming races.

"Okay, Grace, your turn," said Mrs. Mellor.

I'd worked hard on my flip turns in Thailand with my coach and he'd told me they were technically very good, but I was scared of trying it out now in front of Felissia in case she thought I was showing off. In my heart though, I wanted to show Mrs. Mellor what I could do. In the end I decided to go for it, but I was so tense that it didn't turn out very well after all. In fact I probably just looked silly.

"Well done, Grace," said Mrs. Mellor when I got back, which made me feel a little happier. "Bella, your turn."

Bella is a really strong swimmer. I noticed that before Christmas, when we occasionally swam during the weekend for fun. She's much bigger and taller than me and seems to cut through the water like a torpedo as she swims. That word, *torpedo*, made me do a little shudder with the memory of what I'd seen on Georgie's computer. I glanced at Felissia and she flicked her head around, sensing me looking. Our eyes met for a second, then we both turned away and I concentrated on watching Bella's turn. I think she was trying to do a flip turn but, like mine, it didn't quite work out, and slowed her down.

"Nice try, Bella," said Mrs. Mellor. "Hannah, would you like to go next?"

Hannah and Bella are really close friends. They're both from Willowhaven House and I don't think I've ever seen them apart. Hannah is even bigger and stronger than Bella and she swam amazingly powerfully, which made me worry that I was too small and thin. I knew I had a lot of work to do to reach their standard. When Hannah reached the other side she didn't attempt a flip turn, and neither did the next girl, but the last girl in the group, Cassie, who's a friend of Felissia's, did a good one.

"Okay, does anyone have a comment to make about that?" Mrs. Mellor asked.

"Um…I tried to do a flip turn but it didn't really work…" said Bella.

"Don't worry! At least you had a shot at it!" Mrs. Mellor smiled. "And flip turns are the best way to turn around if you're doing front crawl…"

"But for breaststroke it's a two-handed touch, isn't it?" said Felissia.

"That's right," said Mrs. Mellor. "We'll come to that later. For now, I'd like you all to watch Grace again and notice how she breaks into the flip as a continuation of her stroke when she's about a meter away, planting both feet firmly on the wall for a vigorous push-off."

My heart sank. If only she'd chosen Felissia. I was sure Felissia's turn was better than mine. I didn't dare look to see how she was reacting, I just set off nervously. Surprisingly, my flip turn worked a little better the second time though, and afterward everyone had a turn. I was relieved when Felissia managed to do a perfect one right away, and I decided impulsively to try and be friendly. "That was really good, Felissia! Much better than mine!"

The moment I'd spoken I regretted it, because she didn't even bother to reply, let alone smile. It must have sounded as though I thought I was something special and I hoped I hadn't made matters even worse. But then I remembered what Naomi had said, that the message could have been from anyone and might not have been aimed at me at all, and I gave myself a sharp scolding for thinking about it so often instead of concentrating on swimming.

After all the four groups had had a turn at the deep end with Mrs. Mellor, we were allowed to do free swimming, and I noticed Hannah and Bella plowing up and down, doing length after length, not seeming to get at all tired. I knew it would take an awful lot of work for me to be as good as them. Felissia stayed at the shallow end and showed her other best friend, Stella, how to do a flip turn. I didn't think Stella was all that interested because she never tried one out herself, but Felissia just kept doing more and more, and I realized she was actually great at them.

My legs were a bit shaky as I walked back through to the changing room with Jess and the others. Still, I'd survived the lesson, even though I'd been dreading it, and now I was filled with determination to come back on both the weekend days and train like crazy. When I got inside the changing room, though, it was more than just my legs that started to feel shaky. Mrs. Mellor was picking up my bag from the floor, with my school skirt poking out of it. She pursed her lips and said, "Whose is this?"

"M...mine, but...I'm certain I left it on the bench."

A look of puzzlement crept over Mrs. Mellor's face. "Oh dear, Grace..." She paused and I knew she was thinking that she had to take the credits away from me, and maybe she was wondering whether that would be too harsh. My heart beat faster as I waited.

"I did warn them all," said Miss Snow quietly, meeting Mrs. Mellor's eyes. It was a horrible moment, because the changing room was completely silent and I could feel lots of pairs of eyes on me.

"You obviously left your bag too near the edge of the bench, Grace," said Mrs. Mellor. She looked a little sad as she went on and I wondered whether she really believed what she'd just said. "I'm afraid I'll have to take two of the credits away. I think that's the fairest thing...so you and Jemma and Katy get one credit each."

I nodded and tried not to turn red as I took the bag from her and took my towel out to dry myself. I was thinking back to what had happened before I'd rushed through to the swimming pool, and I knew I'd been careful to put the bag right to the back of the bench. I was also sure I'd pushed my skirt in all the way. I could feel myself getting upset as I got dressed, but then told myself firmly to forget it. I'd still gotten one credit, after all, and I hadn't been expecting any before swimming started.

My friends didn't say anything about it at first because they probably didn't want me to feel embarrassed, but when we were back at Hazeldean,

Jess suddenly came out with, "I don't get it, Grace. You're always so organized and tidy."

The others nodded, so it was obvious they knew what Jess was talking about, and Georgie then said exactly what I'd been wondering.

"Do you think someone deliberately knocked it off the bench?" She narrowed her eyes. "Like… Felissia?"

"I don't know, but it doesn't matter," I quickly said.

I felt five pairs of eyes on me and realized I'd spoken quite snappily. I couldn't help it. I knew this conversation was about to lead back to that chat-room message and I was still trying my best to forget about that.

"Maybe someone did it by accident," said Mia, "and didn't realize."

"Mrs. Mellor looked kind of puzzled, though, Grace, didn't she?" Katy said.

Sweet Jess must have seen the tense look on my face. "Let's change the subject," she said. "How did the flip turns go? We saw you all practicing them."

"Fine," I said, keeping my sigh inside, because this wasn't a big enough change of conversation for me to forget about Felissia.

Jess knows me so well that she must have realized I was still anxious. "Oh yes," she said brightly, "I forgot to tell you, I had a plan about spring break. I thought I'd ask Mom if you can come to our house instead of staying with your guardians. My big brother's staying with one of his friends and Mom and Dad'll both be out at work so we'll have the house to ourselves!" Jess's green eyes, which are normally very dreamy, were really sparkling and she looked so pretty with her curly coppery hair.

"That'd be great! I'll just have to check with Mom."

I was going to go home to Thailand for all the long holidays, like Christmas, but it's nearly eighteen hours each way on the plane, so for the short breaks I stay with my guardians in the States. I've known Jan and Pete for ages because they made friends with our family when they came on vacation to Thailand years ago, and we've met up lots of times since. They're both really nice and I knew they were planning a trip to Chicago over spring break, but I still preferred the thought of being with Jess.

After study hour that evening I made my way to the computer room at Hazeldean. I've had to get used to calling it study hour instead of homework, but I don't mind the way we do it at Silver Spires, sitting silently in a room with one of the house staff supervising. Jess had already texted her mom to ask about me staying for spring break, but we hadn't heard back from her, which Jess said wasn't surprising because her mom's an accountant and often gets home late from work. I thought it was somewhat of an important thing to ask my own mom in a text, so I'd decided to e-mail her, and make it a nice newsy one.

Georgie was the only other person in the room and I couldn't help feeling a little nervous when I realized she was chatting online.

"Don't look so worried, Grace," she said. "It's been a whole week since that last message." Her eyes went straight back to the screen. "I don't know who on earth this is online at the moment, but she certainly knows some good jokes!"

I sat down at the next-door computer and looked at my watch. It would be early in the morning in Thailand so my parents would be getting ready for work and wouldn't look at my e-mail until they got back from work in the evening. That didn't matter though. I typed away, telling them all about today's swimming lesson, concentrating on how my Christmas vacation training sessions had definitely paid off, because I knew that would please Mom and

Dad. Then I told them about the history lesson when Mr. Wilson had praised the essay I'd done the night before. I left it until the very end to ask about staying with Jess for spring break. And only after I'd pressed send did I look at Georgie and see that she was staring at her screen with a look of major concentration on her face.

My heart beat a little bit faster. "What's up, Georgie?"

She didn't speak, so I got up and read what was written on her screen over her shoulder, but it didn't make sense because it just said, *Don't you think?*

"What's that mean?" I asked her.

Her voice sounded suddenly weak. "Have you seen who's written it?"

I read the username that she was pointing to. *One credit too many.*

And something tightened in my stomach.

Chapter Three

"Text from Mom!" said Jess, when we all met up in the courtyard at morning break the next day. "Let's see what she says."

It had been such a disappointment the previous evening when Jess's mom had called her just before bedtime to say she was sorry but she had to work all through the spring break week with only one day off in the middle, so Jess was going to be spending the daytimes with her twin cousins who were in elementary school, and their mom, Jess's Aunt Lyn.

"Daisy and Emma are perfectly nice," Jess had said with a sigh, "but they don't like doing the same things as me. They're into magazines and horoscopes, and they're happy to just sit in their bedroom with the TV on, but I prefer...you know...exploring with my camera."

But then today at breakfast she'd suddenly come up with a solution. "I could ask Mom if you can come to Aunty Lyn's too! I'm sure she wouldn't mind." She giggled. "We could escape the twins and go off for walks together!"

So now we were both desperate to see what Jess's mom thought about that idea.

I knew it wasn't going to be good news from the face Jess was making as she read the text. "Oh no! Mom says she doesn't like to ask Aunty Lyn to be responsible for an extra person, and that she'd prefer to be around herself when you come to stay anyway. She's going on about the Easter break, but you'll be going home then, won't you?"

"Well, *you* might be able to stay with me in Thailand over Easter!" I said, feeling excited again.

"Never mind Easter!" said Georgie. "What about this afternoon? Who's coming on the shopping trip? I've still got to buy presents for the Chinese New Year weekend."

Every few months there's an international evening or weekend, when some or all of the six houses get together to put on games and activities, as well as a special dinner. In the spring it's always a Chinese evening, to celebrate the Chinese New Year that falls sometime in January or February. This year it was in February. It was very exciting building up to it because traditionally everyone buys their friends little gifts, and the seventh graders told us that the house staff also buys something small for every single girl in the house. I'd already bought my gifts, over the holidays, and had them stashed away at the back of my drawer in my box of precious things.

It turned out that everyone wanted to go shopping except me and Jess, who was planning on spending the afternoon with her camera. Personally, I'd been hoping to go to the pool to practice my breathing for my front crawl, but an anxious feeling had started to well up inside me about being on my own, in case Felissia was there.

Jess must have read my mind. "Actually I'd like to go to the pool. It might be the one and only time I get to do any floating!"

"No, don't worry," I quickly said. "I'll be all right." Then I found myself blurting out my fears. "I just wish I'd never seen those messages. It's awful knowing someone doesn't like me but not knowing who."

"You mustn't let it get to you," said Naomi, "because that's exactly what this horrible person wants. Remember, you've got to act normally, as though nothing's bothering you. And there's still a chance that the messages are nothing to do with you, anyway. After all, Georgie's got about seventy sixth graders on her contact list and there were only eighteen of us in the swimming lesson yesterday!"

The others nodded their heads in agreement, but it was obvious they were only trying to cheer me up, because how could *One credit too many* be aimed at anyone else but me?

"You didn't reply, did you, Georgie?" asked Mia, suddenly.

Georgie shook her head. "No, but maybe next time they're online I ought to tell them that Grace thinks they're pathetic and so do I. Then perhaps they won't bother us any more."

"No, don't!" I quickly said. "That might make them do something worse. I'd rather just try and ignore it."

Jess looked thoughtful. "Perhaps if it happens again, Georgie, you ought to type something like, *You're wasting your time writing stuff about Grace because I'm purposely not telling her any of it.*"

"No," I protested again, "because they'll find other ways of…getting at me."

"It's actually bullying," said Jess. "I think you should report it, Grace."

"But what would I say? I don't know who it is and it doesn't sound all that terrible calling yourself *One credit too many* and saying, *Don't you think?* And even if a teacher found out who said it, which is impossible, that person could pretend they were talking about something else entirely."

Mia seemed to agree with Jess. "What about that first message, though? That was horrible."

I was feeling more and more uncomfortable because it was too hard to explain why I didn't want any teachers involved. Yes, I was scared that whoever had it in for me would be angry if she found out I'd told a teacher. But there was another reason. Before Christmas, my really precious stopwatch had been stolen, and Ms. Carmichael, the principal, had had to make an announcement about it in assembly and eventually I'd gotten it back. But I don't want the teachers to think I'm always in the middle of a drama. They might get fed up with me.

"Look, I'm fine, honestly," I said, smiling brightly even though it was the last thing I felt like doing. "Naomi's right. I've just got to act like nothing's bothering me, then they'll leave me alone."

"All the same, I'm coming swimming with you," said Jess. "There's loads of time for me to take a few pictures as well afterwards."

I was determined to stand on my own two feet, though, and I couldn't let poor Jess spend her Saturday afternoon swimming when she'd so much rather be out with her beloved camera. "Jess, I'll be fine. I promise."

There was no one in the changing room but there were loads of bags and clothes and shoes lying around the place, which meant that the pool was going to be pretty crowded. I didn't recognize any of the shoes. Some were boots, but most were sneakers of all different colors. What did Felissia wear on her feet? I had no idea. *Stop thinking about it, Grace,* I told myself sharply. Anyway, there was always at least one lifeguard at the pool so who could hurt me?

Hurt me? I really had to get rid of these ridiculous ideas. All that had happened was a few nasty words written on a computer. No one wanted to hurt me. They didn't even dare reveal who they were. They were hiding behind the computer screen. Why should I worry about such weak people?

Instead of wrapping the towel around my shoulders I hung it around my neck, so I wouldn't be as tempted to hug it to me like a kind of security blanket. Then I made myself go through to the pool. The warm air met me, which felt comforting, and I was glad to hear so much noise too. That meant everyone was having fun and no one would pay any attention to me. I put the towel on one of the rails at the side, feeling a little lost without it, and ran my eyes as casually as I could over the pool. The only person I could clearly make out was Hannah. She was doing front crawl, cutting through the water with her head down, and only breathing on every third stroke. I so hoped Mrs. Mellor would teach us the proper front crawl technique on the swim team.

I didn't like standing on the edge – it made me feel really conspicuous – but I badly wanted to know if Felissia was in the pool, before I got in. I'd just feel more secure if I knew that, so I pretended to be adjusting my goggles and then tucking bits of stray hair into my swimming cap, which gave me a chance to take a better look. The only other person I instantly recognized was Bella, at the deep end with her back to the wall, her arms stretched out along the rail, her eyes on me. I quickly looked away, then sat down on the edge and twisted my body around

41

as I slid in, so no one would see me wince at the chill of the water. I really wanted to swim hard up and down the pool, trying to get faster at front crawl and concentrate on the breathing, but I couldn't be sure that no one was watching me, and I didn't want to attract too much attention. What I really mean is, I couldn't be sure that Felissia wasn't watching me.

It annoyed me that I even cared whether she was watching or not, but I knew I wouldn't be able to relax until I'd found out if she was actually in the pool. To give myself a little more time, I pretended to be warming up, rolling my shoulders and drawing my knees up to my chest one at a time. Then I stopped abruptly at the sound of a snicker. I couldn't tell who it was, but it made me spring into action and start swimming.

At least with breaststroke, unless you're doing it with the proper technique and dipping your face in on every stroke, you can look around a bit. So that's what I did and it didn't take any time at all for me to spot Felissia, Stella and Cassie doing handstands near the shallow end. My stomach knotted immediately. Bella and Hannah were practicing flip turns a little farther up, and a group of seventh graders were plowing up and down the pool in pairs. A bunch of sixth graders were having a hold-your-breath-underwater competition. I must have been the only person on my own. Maybe I should have said "Yes please" when Jess offered to come. But no one seemed to be looking at me, except the lifeguard, and she was only looking because that was her job.

After four lengths of nice comfortable breaststroke, I gave myself a firm scolding. *Okay, Grace, stop being silly and get on with what you came to do.* So I changed to front crawl and really tried to push myself to go as fast as I could. I made up the rule that I wasn't allowed to stop until I'd done eight lengths, but by the time I'd done four I was wishing I'd made it six, because my muscles were tight and I'd already slowed down a lot. It was also more difficult because the pool was so crowded, so I made a resolution to turn up before breakfast the next day. Then, with some luck, I'd get the pool all to myself. I don't mind the thought of being on my own. In fact I prefer it, because I can concentrate on my training without worrying about anyone watching, apart from the lifeguard.

At the end of the eight lengths I felt exhausted and wished I'd set myself the task of doing an odd number, as then I could have finished at the deep end where the water would go right up to my neck. I felt stupid in the shallow end, because I had to bend my legs until I was nearly kneeling to make sure my top half wasn't sticking up out of the water. When I wasn't out of breath any more I went under and peered around through my goggles. Everything sounded muffled and unreal, and it was weird to see pale legs kicking and flapping in slow motion. In a funny way it made me feel calm and safe, but after a while I ran out of breath and had to come up again, where the shrill echoey sounds of chatter and laughter hit me like an alarm clock going off.

This time I took a real look around and was surprised to see no sign of Felissia and her friends. Bella and Hannah were still practicing flip turns near the deep end. I decided to try one myself, so I swam to the side about halfway up the pool and pushed hard down into the somersault. It worked really well and I managed to keep swimming underwater all the way up to the other side of the pool. I came up gasping and happy, then turned to see both Bella and Hannah staring at me, so I quickly looked away. A moment later they got out too and after a while there was only me and a few seventh graders left. I felt much more comfortable without anyone from my year in the pool, and even better when I saw through the massive window behind the lifeguard's tall chair that Felissia and her friends were rushing off somewhere, swinging their bags and laughing. It's funny how easily you can see out from the inside. If the sun's shining and you're looking in from outside you can't see anything except reflections.

I enjoyed myself for the next twenty minutes, swimming up and down and timing myself by the giant clock on the wall, and by the time I got out of the pool I had that nice satisfied feeling I always get after training. I couldn't say I was looking forward to swim team, but at least I wasn't worried any more, because Felissia hadn't done anything horrible to me in the pool. Okay, she hadn't exactly been friendly, but then we didn't know each other particularly well and, anyway, she'd just been messing around with her friends, and there was nothing wrong with that.

When I got up to the dorm it was a nice surprise to find Jess there, looking at photos on her digital camera.

"I've taken some really good ones," she said, in what I call her faraway voice. "I'm going to edit them on the computer later." Then she looked at me and saw my wet hair. "Oh! Sorry! How was swimming? Was Felissia there?"

"Yes, but she was fine. She didn't say anything or give me any funny looks or spoil my training at all, so I'm not worried any more. I think I've gotten a little faster at front crawl, too, but I want to get much much faster in time for the competition. Hannah's great at it."

Jess's dreamy look changed to a sparkly one and I could tell she was relieved that nothing awful had happened to me. When the others got back from shopping we all went to make hot chocolate in the kitchen, then took it up to the dorm and played twenty questions sitting on the round rug. It was pouring down outside, which always gives me a nice cozy feeling. Katy had bought a big red shift dress in a thrift store, but she was being a little secretive about it.

"I don't get what you want it for," said Georgie, wrinkling her nose. "It's ten times too big for you."

Katy smiled. "Aha! You shall see!"

Everyone seemed pleased to hear that my training had been fine, and after we'd watched some TV and had dinner, Jess and I went to look at her photos on one of the computers. The first one was of a sash window that was slightly open, and showed the bottom of a net curtain that had blown underneath the window and gotten dirty with the rain and the dust from the window. Then, as she showed me the rest, I realized they were all of windows, but every one was completely different, some looking out and some looking in.

"I like thinking about this," she told me, with a distant look in her eyes. "Are we the outsiders looking in, or are the outsiders the ones inside, looking out like prisoners?"

It's great talking with Jess about things like that and I asked her if she'd ever thought of photographing the swimming-pool window.

"That's a good idea," she said thoughtfully. "I'd probably get some interesting reflections. But then I might not get anything else except reflections, unless the sun wasn't shining...only then there wouldn't be enough light..."

"What about if you did it from inside?"

"Then I think I'd get detention!" she laughed. "I'm not sure that cameras are allowed at the poolside – Mrs. Mellor would think I'm nuts!"

"What's so funny?" asked Georgie, coming in at that moment and going straight online.

When we told her she laughed too, but then the laughter died away and I instantly knew why.

"It's another message, isn't it?" I said heavily. "Let me see."

This time when I read the words I felt like bursting into tears.

Don't choo-choo skinny gal cos skinny = useless = loser

"It's from *Torpedo Gal*," said Jess sadly. She turned away.

"Wh…what's *choo-choo*?" I asked shakily.

"Train," said Georgie quietly. "She's telling you not to train."

I could feel myself going all crumbly inside, but I wanted to stay strong because the moment I showed fear one of my friends would be sure to go to a teacher. "How do you know she means…me? I'm not…the only skinny one." But even as I was saying it I was remembering how I'd stood on the side for a while fiddling with my goggles and swimming cap so I could try to see if Felissia was in the pool. Perhaps it had looked like I was showing off. I flopped down into the seat beside Jess, as a horrible thought suddenly occurred to me. I blurted it out, because it felt too shocking to keep inside. "I don't think it *is* Felissia, you know."

"What!" said Georgie, swinging her head around.

My mind was zooming back over the whole swimming session, taking snapshots along the way… Bella staring at me with her arms stretched out along the rail. Hannah and Bella practicing flip turns. Me doing a perfect one. The way they looked at me, then got out almost immediately after.

"Think about it…" I said dully. "Felissia's not much different in height and shape from me. But Bella and Hannah are miles bigger. Why should Felissia say anything about me being skinny?" I hung my head. "And they were practicing flip turns and I just stupidly went and did a perfect one. They must have thought I was a total show-off. I wish I hadn't done it. It's my own fault."

Jess's eyes were wide with shock. "You can't blame yourself, Grace! *They're* the evil ones. *And* they're threatening you!" She bit her lip. "I mean… whoever it is…"

"Yes," said Georgie, looking just as put out as Jess. "Whoever it is, they've got the nerve to tell you not to train. Huh!"

The door opened and we all jumped for no reason except that the message had made us tense.

"It's only me! Not a ghost!" said Mia, trying to make us smile. But a second later she realized we were deadly serious. "Wh…what's happened?"

"Tell you in the dorm," said Jess flatly.

So a few minutes later, as we were all getting ready for bed, I explained about the message to Mia, Naomi and Katy.

"Whoever it is, it's definitely *their* problem, not yours," said Naomi, looking cross.

"Don't you think Grace ought to report it?" asked Georgie, eyes flashing.

"The teachers would be furious if they knew that people were using the chat room for this kind of thing," Katy said.

"Exactly! And they'd probably ban it," I pointed out. "Then if people found out it was thanks to me, they'd hate me!" I shivered without meaning to. "I really don't want to report it," I said, turning to Naomi and talking to her in a panicky gabble like she was my mom. "Remember you said I shouldn't let it bother me, Naomi?"

She nodded slowly, her big eyes staring into the distance as though she could remember saying it, but wasn't quite so convinced about it any more. Jess put her arm around me and I took a deep breath. I was trying to be so brave and strong, but inside I was turning to jelly.

Chapter Four

It wasn't easy keeping my nerve until swim team on Wednesday. Whenever I was anywhere near the main building, it was tempting to rush in and erase my name off the list, but I knew that if I did that one of my friends would try and explain everything to Miss Carol or Mrs. Mellor. Each time Georgie went on the computer I felt myself tensing right up, because I was sure it would only take one more horrible message aimed at me before one of them went right ahead and reported it. And there was another reason why I didn't want to show how worried I really felt, too; because if I lost my nerve

I might never get it back and then I'd be so disappointed in myself. My parents had brought me up to face up to things and always to try my best and never give in. And that's what I was doing right now, even though it felt like the hardest test I'd ever had in my life.

"Remember," said Jess, catching my tense look as I was about to set off to the pool, "Mrs. Mellor will be there, *and* Miss Snow and the lifeguard..." Her eyes flashed. "So if Bella or Hannah say anything nasty or threatening to you, you just tell someone right away, okay?"

Now I felt as though *Jess* was my mom. I tried to make my voice as light as possible. "It'll be fine, I'm sure."

There were twenty of us on the swim team and we got changed on our own while Mrs. Mellor sorted things out in the pool area. I was chatting with a girl named Evie from Oakley House, who's really bubbly and reminds me a little of Georgie. I made doubly sure I pushed my clothes deep into my bag this time and left the bag right at the very back of the bench. Then I wrapped myself in my towel and sat on the bench waiting for Evie, feeling strange and isolated even with all the chatter going on around me.

"Grace, *you're* ready," said Mrs. Mellor, appearing

suddenly and bringing me out of my daydream. "Off you go."

As soon as I got to the pool area I went straight down the steps, not even noticing whether the water was cold or not. I did backstroke to the other end, being careful to keep looking over my shoulder to make sure I wasn't about to bash into anyone, then I did breaststroke back to the shallow end because by then Bella and Hannah were in the pool, swimming back and forth across the deep end, and Felissia was lying on her back right in the middle with her eyes closed, getting her friend to pull her around. Cassie was laughing away.

After a few minutes of warm-up, Mrs. Mellor jumbled up all the different houses into five teams for a medley relay, and told us which lane to line up by at the deep end. I wasn't put with Bella or Hannah *or* Felissia, thank goodness, but I did have Evie on my team, so that felt like a good omen.

"Grace ought to go last if it's a relay," Evie said. "You're always supposed to put your fastest swimmer last."

"Well I'm not all that fast actually," I quickly said, but no one seemed to be listening because the other three had already arranged themselves in front of me, so it went: Nicole, Evie, Holly, me.

Looking at the team in the next lane I noticed Felissia was also at the back, standing level with me, which meant that she and I would be competing against each other. But I didn't mind that at all now I was pretty sure she wasn't the one sending the messages. Bella and Hannah were in lane one, which was the farthest away from my team, thank goodness, but my heart jittered when I saw that Hannah was also swimming last for her team.

"Everyone should swim two lengths. Those swimming first, you must do breaststroke, the girls in second place swim backstroke, those in third, freestyle, and the girls swimming last, front crawl. Got that?" said Mrs. Mellor. "Today you can choose whether you want to start in the water, or dive in from the block or just from the side. Next week we'll do proper diving technique using the blocks, in preparation for the competition, but for now, whether or not you decide to dive in, you must make sure that the person before you in your team touches the wall before you set off, and if they're doing breaststroke they must touch with both hands. Those of you in first position in your team who want to dive in, be careful not to dive before my whistle, or it's a false start. If I see anyone do a false start, I'll blow the whistle repeatedly right afterwards

to tell you to start again. Okay, everyone ready?"
Mrs. Mellor waited for silence, then said, "On your
marks..." and blew her whistle.

I was glad I wasn't going first because I would
have been so worried about doing a false start that
I'd have probably dived in late, which would have
put the team behind right away. But the first four
girls all dived in or set off from the side perfectly on
the whistle, and right away everyone started calling
out, "Come on!" to their team members, until the
pool area was full of shrill noise and echoes. All four
teams stayed more or less level until the second
people set off. Evie was doing backstroke, but kept
going off course and having to wiggle her way back
into the middle of the lane, so by the time it was
Holly's turn we were coming level last with Hannah's
team. Holly managed to get the tiniest bit ahead of
the third girl on Hannah's team so I dived in just
before Hannah, but in no time at all she was ahead
of me, beating her arms against the water and
driving herself forward. Half of me wanted to use
every single atom of energy I possessed to try and
catch up with her, but the other half of me was
holding back, scared of what I might see on the
computer later.

Hannah touched the side at the deep end before

I went into my flip turn, but I kicked hard off the wall and when I came up I found I'd managed to draw level with her, and that was when my competitive spirit suddenly flooded in and made me determined to beat her. Felissia had already finished so her team had won, and I knew from Mrs. Mellor's whistles that the other teams had finished too, which just left my team and Hannah's. I flung my arms out as hard as I could with every stroke and tried to get the breathing right, though it didn't really work. Everyone was yelling out to us excitedly at the tops of their voices and even though it sounded strange and muffled with my head down, it made me try even harder. Two more strokes to go. Then one. My fingers touched the side and a single whistle sounded.

"Dead heat!" cried Mrs. Mellor. Her face was all shiny and smiling. "Well done, both of you!"

I looked across at Hannah and our eyes met. I would have definitely managed a smile if she'd given me one, but she instantly looked away and I felt the energy leaving my body. I tried to get out of the pool, but it was a struggle because my arms seemed to have totally lost their strength. Evie and the others laughed as they hauled me out, congratulating me at the same time, which made me feel better.

"Great job, Grace! You were amazing!"

"Like a torpedo!" said Evie, her voice raised in a high-pitched squeal.

Why did that word keep popping up? Immediately, some of my high spirits fizzled away. Mrs. Mellor snapped everyone back to attention with a shrill blast on her whistle, then made a few comments about how we'd done. "It's not long until the competition now, girls, so we need to spend some time working on weak areas. I'll be coming around to give individual help, because every one of you here today will be swimming in the competition – some more than others. I haven't decided yet exactly which races you'll all be competing in but I'll let you know in due course."

That was just what I needed to pull myself out of my depression, because it was exciting to imagine which races I might be entered in and I wanted to sort out my breathing for front crawl. But thinking about the competition also filled me with butterflies, and I had to work hard on my breathing technique for the rest of the session to make my nervousness go away.

Later, I told the others that swim team had been fine and I'd even managed to keep up with Hannah in a race over two lengths. I didn't mention the look that she and I had exchanged at the end, which should have been a smile but was actually no more than the briefest, emptiest stare.

Jess must have felt my unease. "Oh, by the way, I had the most obvious idea in the world during art club. If Georgie stops going online, then whoever it is won't bother sending any messages. Simple!" She turned her palms up and smiled around at us all.

"I don't know why we didn't think of that before!" said Naomi, grinning back at Jess. "It's true that Georgie only has to keep out of the chat room till after the swimming competition, and everything will be fine."

I knew I should have been happy with this idea, but it was just making me worry all the more. Seeing those horrible messages had been really upsetting, but the thought of not seeing them and wondering whether or not I was being talked about seemed ten times worse. And the worst thing of all...what if then the chat-room messages turned into real live bullying?

"Just one small thing, guys..." said Georgie. "I hate to point it out to you all, but if I'm going to be banned from using the chat room, and as I don't have a million and one things to do, like all of you, aren't I going to get a teensy bit bored?"

"It's true, it's not fair on poor old Georgie!" I quickly said.

"I've got a good idea," said Katy, in an excited gabble. "Why don't you change your username, Georgie? Then no one will know whether you're online or not."

"Great!" said Jess. "Let's help Georgie invent a new username. What's your old one?"

"*Castles in the Air*," Georgie answered promptly, with a proud look on her face. "I couldn't resist having the name of the play before Christmas. *And,* get this, my clever username also helps me to remember my password, which is '*bouncy* castle'! How cool is that?" She suddenly looked a little alarmed. "If I have to change it, I really want something to do with drama, you know."

"Don't worry, we'll think of something just as good," said Katy encouragingly.

So the decision was made for us all to think of ideas until study hour had finished, then get together and see what we'd come up with. My five friends spent most of dinner staring into space with frowns on their faces, and I knew they were concentrating on coming up with a great new username and password for Georgie, but personally I was in a state because Hannah and Bella were at the next table and I could just feel their eyes on me, which made me shiver inside.

Walking over to Hazeldean after dinner, I suddenly had a brainwave out of the blue and I didn't know why I hadn't thought of it before. It was a relief to be thinking of something that had nothing at all to do with messages or swimming for a change.

"Why don't I ask Jan if it's okay for you to spend spring break with *me*, Jess? I'm sure she won't mind. Then you'd get to come to Chicago and everything."

"Wow, that would be awesome!" said Jess. So I rushed off to e-mail Jan right away before study hour.

I usually enjoy study hour because it gives me a nice calm feeling being with all my friends, silently working away. It was math this evening, which is one of my favorite subjects. Jess needed some help so I did her first couple of questions for her, but then she got the hang of it and managed the rest on her own. If it had been Miss Fosbrook on duty she wouldn't have minded my helping Jess so much, but Miss Carol is much stricter and makes us work completely on our own for the whole hour, so I had to be careful not to let her notice what I was doing. Usually, I don't like breaking rules like that. But some things are more important than rules. Like friendship.

As we were finishing study hour, Katy slid a piece of paper across the table to me with the words *William Shakespeare* on it. She raised her eyebrows as if to ask me what I thought of it, and I gave her a thumbs up, then went back to checking my math. I couldn't concentrate though. Those two little words had jolted me right back into that chat-room world. The world of my fears.

Afterwards on the way up to the dorm, Georgie wrinkled her nose. "*William Shakespeare?* It's not very original, is it? Anyway, what would my password be?"

"*Shake it!*" said Katy.

"Awesome, Katy!" said Naomi. "What's wrong with that, Georgie?"

Georgie sighed a massive sigh. "I just really like my old username. Look, let's go back to plan A. I'll give up messaging for a while, okay?" She broke into a grin. "Now for important things. Who's coming to flop onto a nice soft beanbag and watch TV with me?"

We were all laughing as we set off along to the common room, but once we were there and had sunk into the sofas and beanbags everyone fell quiet. I tried to concentrate on the program, but my mind kept wandering because something was niggling away at me. What if Hannah and Bella were busy typing horrible things about me right now? They probably weren't, as Georgie wasn't online. But what if they *were*? What if there were other people joining in their conversation, all dissing me as I lay here on this beanbag.

Suddenly I had to know. And I realized I could easily find out. After all, I knew Georgie's password now. *Bouncy castle.* And I already knew her e-mail address because we'd all e-mailed each other over Christmas. I could go online and pretend to be her. I didn't have to make it into a big deal and tell my friends. Once the idea had taken root in my mind I couldn't let it go.

"Back in a minute," I whispered to Jess.

She nodded without taking her eyes off the screen and I didn't think the others even noticed that I was leaving the room, they were so into the program. All the same, I knew I had to be quick in case one of them decided to come along to the computer room and e-mail their parents. We often e-mail at this time of evening before bedtime.

My hands were shaking as I typed in Georgie's password and saw the list of people who were online. There were five of them and I only recognized one of their usernames. Someone called *x little emms x* was probably Emma Horn from Forest Ash, because she's very small. A moment after I'd signed in there came a message from *Helen of Troy*, who might have been Helen Banister from Willowhaven or Helen Sukra from Elmhurst or another Helen. She wrote, *Any1 got any nail p remoo?*

Someone called *Dreads* wrote, *Soz babz.* Then someone else wrote, *Yo. Givit ya 2moz.* The conversation went on to different nail polish colors and shades and I noticed that after that quite a few usernames seemed to have colors in them, like *Scarlet Pimpernel* and *Bluebell Woods,* which made me realize how people sometimes changed their usernames according to the conversation they were having. I kept on thinking I ought to be writing something myself otherwise the other people who were online might think it a little strange, but I couldn't decide what Georgie would write. Instead, I clicked on *Away*, so then people would think I'd had to go away from the computer for a while. After that the conversation changed to swimming and I held my breath waiting for a nasty comment. *Torpedo Gal* wasn't online, but of course Hannah or Bella might have changed their usernames.

It was good at swim team, someone named *Evita* wrote, and I suddenly wondered whether it was

Evie. I couldn't understand why people liked messaging so much when half the time they didn't even know who they were talking to. The next message to come up was from *Razzle Tazzle*. She wrote, *Din u av nuff torture last Fri? Y turn up 4 more? Evita* replied, *Luv ya but ur a wimp. I was worthless. My team came dead last, but I still* ♥ *it.*

Now my heart was racing furiously because I was so sure that any minute I'd see a message about the show-off who did the flip turn or the girl who couldn't even get out of the pool on her own, or something like that, but nothing came, and the subject changed to a discussion about TV programs. Then everyone started saying *Bi* and *Nite* to each other, and *Watch the bugs don't bite* and *Quik! Dorm mom alert!* which made me realize I had to sign out and get up to the dorm before someone found me. I'd been lucky to have the whole computer room to myself for so long, but it's true that on Wednesday evenings there are good TV programs on, so most people go to the common room after study hour.

"Where did you go off to?" asked Jess, looking confused, as soon as I went into the dorm.

I had my reply ready, although I didn't like lying to Jess, even if it was only a small one.

"I went to see if Jan had replied to my e-mail, but she hadn't, so then I e-mailed my sister."

Thinking about my sister sent a pang of homesickness whizzing around my body, but only for a second, because I was so relieved that there hadn't been any nasty messages and I could actually relax.

We have to hand in our phones every night to Miss Jennings's office and we'd all picked a day of the week to be phone monitor, but on Sundays it was a free-for-all. Tonight was Mia's turn, and I was just about to switch mine off and hand it over when it rang.

"Oh hi, Jan!" I said, which made Jess shush everyone so she could listen.

It was great to hear Jan's voice. She always sounds so bright and bubbly. And it was even nicer to hear what she was saying. "Of course I'd love for your friend to come for the week, Grace. I just need to be sure that it's all right with her parents."

I didn't think there'd be a problem with Jess's parents but I wanted to give Jess a nice surprise at the end of the call, so I kept my voice level and said, "I'm not sure. We were just asking you first."

Jess opened her eyes wide and raised her open palms, as if to say, *What's happening?* But I turned my back and continued talking with Jan for another minute, being careful not to give anything away. After I'd said goodbye, I turned around slowly to see Jess bursting with curiosity. Then I smiled and spoke quietly. "Yes! You can come!"

"Yay!" said Jess, giving me a hug. "Just my mom to ask, then it will be settled."

I thought about that as I went off to the bathroom. Jess was right, things did gradually seem to be sorting themselves out. The messages seemed to have stopped, and I had the support of all my amazing friends. Not *everyone* thought I was a show-off. I was cross with myself for having used Georgie's password like that without asking, though. All I'd done was make myself feel nervous at first and guilty afterwards. I wouldn't do it again.

Good decision. And now I had the nice Chinese weekend to look forward to, and then spring break with Jess. Yesssss!

Chapter Five

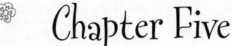

The build-up to the Chinese New Year weekend was nearly as good as the weekend itself. We all had to be responsible for straightening and cleaning our own dorms and one other area of the boarding house, because apparently in China there's a huge clean-up in the days before the New Year to sweep away bad luck. I liked that idea, and really threw myself into my main job, which was polishing our wooden floor in the dorm. I wanted to make absolutely sure there wasn't a single trace of bad luck hanging around anywhere.

Maybe I didn't do it thoroughly enough, or maybe Jess didn't wipe the windowsills very well, because we did get one piece of bad luck. Jess's mom had said she wasn't sure about Jess being away for the entire spring break, but Jess had confidently told me that she could easily get her mom to change her mind. What actually happened, though, was that her mom called to explain that she was sorry but she'd thought about it and she was afraid she'd miss Jess too much, as she'd only get to see her during the main holidays then. Because of having to work during the week, she'd want to have Jess at home for both the weekends and she'd seen from the map that Jan and Peter lived too far away for Jess to travel back and forth. Jess and I were both really disappointed, but Jess did admit that she'd miss her mom and dad too if she didn't get to see them until the Easter holidays, so in the end we had to forget about plans for spring break.

It was a good thing we had Chinese New Year to keep us cheerful. Another tradition in China is decorating your windows and doors with little verses about things like happiness, riches and long life. So we did the same at Silver Spires, decorating our boarding houses with the rhyming couplets we'd had to make up for one of our English assignments.

We'd been told by Miss Carol to dress in as much red as possible on the Saturday evening, and definitely no black, as it's bad luck, or white, because the Chinese associate it with mourning. And when it came to Saturday afternoon Katy gave us all a wonderful surprise by handing each of us a very broad red belt that she called a hip wrap.

"So *that's* why you bought that red dress!" said Georgie.

"I can't believe you made all these!" said Mia. "You're so talented!"

And the rest of us totally agreed.

We wore our hip wraps over our jeans and some of us had more red on our top halves too. I happened to have a red T-shirt, so that was perfect. Katy had the most beautiful red sequined top with floaty sleeves. She also had some fabulous red sneakers. Jess had made red flowers out of paper for our hair. I couldn't make mine stay in because my hair's so straight and fine, so in the end I pinned it to the top of my jeans. Naomi looked absolutely wonderful because she had a red-and-gold silk top *and* matching pants, which she'd brought specially for the Chinese weekend. It seemed strange seeing her so dressed up, because although she's got some beautiful traditional African outfits, she only ever brings one or two of them to school in case she has a photo shoot or something. Normally she just wears jeans and sweat pants and things, like everyone else.

Miss Carol had put up a notice for the sixth, seventh and eighth graders to meet at five o'clock in the common room, because she wanted to talk to us briefly about the swimming competition before the Chinese New Year celebrations started. As my friends and I gathered with the others, everyone wondered what Miss Carol wanted to talk about, since it was supposed to be Mrs. Mellor organizing the swimming competition.

"Now," began Miss Carol. "First for the sixth graders – Mrs. Mellor says that Hazeldean is very well represented for swimmers from the seventh and eighth grades, but she's a little short on sixth graders. In fact we only have Grace, Rhianna and Yasmin. Does anyone else want to volunteer?"

"Mrs. Mellor ought to put Grace in for everything," said one of the eighth graders. "She's like a torpedo!"

My stomach clenched at the sound of the dreaded word, and I quickly looked at the girl who had spoken, but she was smiling at me and giving me a big thumbs up.

"Yea! Go Grace!" said someone else, and my worry dissolved a little. It was nice that people in

Hazeldean seemed to want me to do well for the house, so I didn't have to worry that anyone here thought of me as a show-off. But I still felt anxious, because what if I let my house down? I so wished people would understand that swimming isn't my best sport.

"I can't do it on my own, I really can't!" I said in a panic. "I need Rhianna and Yasmin...and anyone else who wants to join in. There are lots of great swimmers in the other houses."

"Yes, it's true, Beech House has Felissia, don't they?" one of the seventh graders said. "She's the best swimmer in sixth grade."

Another seventh grader joined in. "Then there are those two girls in Willowhaven who hang out together all the time... What are their names?"

"Bella and Hannah," said Naomi.

"That's right. They're amazing."

"So is no one else volunteering?" asked Miss Carol.

There was a silence apart from a few mumbles, and lots of people shook their heads.

"Well think about it and let me know. It'd be great if Hazeldean had a really strong team," said Miss Carol. "On to the next thing, then – the design for the cover of the swimming-competition program.

Every year there's a competition where each house can submit one entry and Ms. Carmichael secretly chooses her favorite design but only tells the other staff. As you know, the competition is an internal event with no parents attending, but all the staff gets a program and at the start of the competition they reveal the front cover, which is always very exciting. The house with the winning design gains five points toward the overall House Cup at the end of spring. An added bonus is that the cover is always printed in the school magazine." Miss Carol flicked her head from side to side, looking over us all to see if anyone was volunteering for the job of designing a front cover, and surprisingly no one seemed interested, if the expressions on the faces of the seventh and eighth graders were anything to go by.

"You ought to do it, Jess," I whispered, and Katy heard me.

"We're volunteering Jess, Miss Carol," she said, grinning.

Jess was staring at the wall and I knew her imagination would be working away.

"Go Jess!" said one of the eighth graders.

"Is that all right with you, Jessica?" asked Miss Carol.

Jess lost the dreamy look in her eyes and nodded. "Okay."

There were more whoops of delight from the older girls, and one of them said she was glad we finally had a good artist in Hazeldean.

Miss Carol smiled. "Excellent. Let's forget all about swimming things now and get on to the reason we're really here. I've written out this evening's special Chinese New Year's Eve menu – feast your eyes on this, girls!" She unrolled a large sheet of yellow paper and tacked it to the wall, and everyone started reading it out loud. Personally I liked the look of the prawns, which were supposed to be for liveliness and happiness, and the raw fish salad to bring good luck. I'm used to eating raw fish at home in Thailand. In fact, it's one of the things I really miss when I'm away at school. But quite a few of the girls weren't too sure about it. That didn't matter though, because there were so many other delicious Chinese dishes.

"After dinner you've got the choice of playing organized games or watching TV," said Miss Fosbrook. "Then we've got a fireworks display on the field."

The whole evening turned out to be such fun that we wished Chinese New Year happened more than once a year. The next day was also great, because we exchanged presents in the dorm before breakfast. My friends all loved the presents I gave them, which were little dragonfly ornaments made of wood, painted in different designs. If you put the hook of the dragonfly's head on your finger it would balance, and you could tap its tail to make it rock up and down. Jess gave us all tiny photos of ourselves that she'd taken and put into frames that she'd made out of wire and shells. They were so sweet. Naomi bought us beautiful scented candles, Mia gave us little journals, Katy's presents were bracelets made out of the same red material as our hip wraps and decorated with a few gold sequins, and Georgie gave us licorice twists.

After breakfast we went around all the other houses saying "Happy Chinese New Year" to as many people as we could, but we missed quite a few because most people were out visiting too. I wondered whether I'd come across Felissia in Beech House or Hannah and Bella in Willowhaven, but I didn't, which was a relief.

The house staff gave us our presents next. Miss Carol and the other two in Hazeldean had bought body glitter for the tenth graders, bath oils for the ninth graders, tiny Chinese lanterns for the eighth graders, sweet little wooden boxes for the seventh graders and miniature Chinese calendars for the sixth graders. It was so kind of them and everyone was thanking them like crazy and giving them hugs.

When that had finished I decided to go swimming, and felt perfectly happy about going on my own. I couldn't wait to get in the pool and start working on my front crawl, trying out the technique of breathing on every third stroke that Mrs. Mellor had now helped me with. As I went into the pool building, I wondered whether I'd be chosen from Hazeldean to do front crawl in the swimming competition, and who might be chosen from the other houses. It would very likely be Felissia from Beech House and Hannah from Willowhaven, but I wasn't certain about Oakley, Forest Ash and Elmhurst.

Just before I went into the changing room I saw that the big noticeboard had been stripped bare, and at the top it now said *SWIMMING COMPETITION* in huge letters. Below that there were three headings: *SIXTH GRADE, SEVENTH GRADE* and *EIGHTH GRADE*, and the space underneath was ready for the lists of competitors for all the different races. On the little noticeboard at the side there was a note about the competition to design the front cover for the competition program and as I read it I was aware of someone walking out of the building behind me. As soon as they'd gone past I turned to see that it was Hannah and Bella, their wet hair dripping down their backs. Good. That meant that I didn't have to put up with them staring at me while I was trying to concentrate on working on my strokes.

I got changed really quickly and did a racing dive straight into the pool from one of the blocks, because I thought it would be good practice for the actual swimming competition. I swam two lengths, then had a quick rest before I did another two, to get used to pacing myself over the distance. There weren't many people in the pool so it was one of the best swims I'd had and I felt really invigorated going back into the changing room. But then something terrible happened. The black sweatshirt I'd been wearing seemed to be missing. I looked all over for it, and checked my bag three times, then under the benches and everywhere, but it had simply disappeared. Someone must have taken it by mistake.

I wrapped my towel around my top half and shivered as I remembered Hannah and Bella leaving the building earlier. Had they come back to the changing room after I'd gone into the pool, and deliberately taken my sweatshirt? No, that was a ridiculous thought. I must be getting paranoid. I sat down heavily. I didn't have any other top. I'd have to walk back to Hazeldean in the cold air with my wet towel around me. Then I'd probably catch a chill. Is that what Hannah and Bella wanted? This time I didn't throw the thought away quite so quickly, and found myself wondering whether this was their way of trying to put me off entering the swimming competition. If only I'd had my phone with me I could have asked Jess to bring another top over.

But actually, thinking about it, it would be better if Jess and the others didn't know anything about this. I could just hear Mia's voice: *This is the last straw, Grace. You've absolutely got to tell Miss Carol what's been going on. And if you don't, I will.* I set off running back to Hazeldean, clutching the towel tightly, my head spinning with thoughts about how I could possibly explain where my sweatshirt was when I got back to the dorm and the others saw me wearing a towel. It wasn't easy running with both hands gripping the towel tight and one hand clutching my bag at the same time, but by the time I went in through the front door I'd managed to work out a story about dropping my sweatshirt on the changing room floor, standing on it with my sneakers on by mistake, and deciding it was so wet and yucky that I'd put it straight in the laundry. I thought the story sounded totally believable, though I hated that I was lying. Again.

I was about to rush upstairs when I stopped in my tracks, because hanging over the bottom of the banister was a sweatshirt. I pulled it off and checked the name tape. There wasn't one. It might have peeled off, because Mom had used the iron-on sort of name tapes in some of my clothes. The label said *extra small*, which was my size, and I was also certain it was mine because it was still quite new-looking. As no one was around, I quickly put the sweatshirt on, then walked upstairs slowly, trying to figure out what must have happened and why.

Black sweatshirts were part of the Silver Spires uniform. Maybe someone had lost their own sweatshirt and gone to see if they'd left it in the swimming changing rooms, then they'd come across mine and made a genuine mistake thinking it was their own? Yes, that was it. It was just a mistake, and nothing for me to worry about. It would be ridiculous to get neurotic about every little innocent thing that happened.

All the same, I wouldn't tell the others. Just to be on the safe side. I broke into a jog as I went up the last two flights of stairs. I didn't want anything to spoil this perfect weekend, so I tried to ignore the little niggling voice at the back of my mind saying, *How could anyone have taken your sweatshirt by mistake, Grace, when it was in your bag with the rest of your things?*

Chapter Six

On Sunday night I did what I'd told myself I wouldn't do again, and went online pretending to be Georgie. I couldn't help it. My mind just wouldn't let me ignore the little voice I was trying so hard to shut out, and the thing with my sweatshirt had stirred up all my worries and bad feelings again. This time I was actually brave enough to write a message: *Chinese N.Y. was cool, wasn't it?* I looked at what I'd written for ages without sending it, though. Would Georgie write something like that? Probably not. I changed it to *Chi NY ws so cool.* As I was sending the message I wondered whether it might be better to come right out and say, *It's Grace here. Someone took my sweatshirt from the changing room this morning and I've got a pretty good idea who it was, and if they think they're putting me off swimming training they're wrong, because I'm just ignoring their pathetic games.*

Imagining myself writing those words somehow made me feel strong and determined again. I didn't dare actually write them, of course, but I stayed online for twenty minutes, joining in with the Chinese New Year chat, because I knew the others were occupied watching *The Hundred Best Comedy Moments Ever*, thinking I was e-mailing photos to my parents from the weekend's celebrations. No nasty messages appeared, thank goodness, and I felt massively relieved when I went to join the others.

The next evening I was tempted to go back online, but Georgie was on the computer so I couldn't. Good old Georgie had been true to her word and not done any chat-room messaging since she promised not to, which made me feel even more guilty for pretending to be her online. These days she just stuck to e-mailing her family and texting her friends.

The following day, though, I made an excuse and went off to the computer room while Georgie was helping a tenth grade girl learn some lines for a play that her drama group was doing. This time there were loads of people online. My stomach tightened when I saw the name *Torpedo Gal.* With shaking fingers I typed, *Hey, wot's new?* And a moment later *Torpedo Gal* wrote: *Yo George, I am a mole and I live in a hole.* I didn't have the faintest clue what she was talking about, but someone called *Huggy Bear* then wrote: *He's got the hole world in his hands!!!* I quickly clicked the *Away* button so they'd think I wasn't getting their messages, because I didn't like not being in on their joke. Next *KerryB*, who must have been Kerry Bennett from Hazeldean, wrote: *Wot u talkn bout?* but then signed out right away. *Torpedo Gal* and *Huggy Bear* didn't say anything else, but shortly after that a new username came up – *Hole heartedly.* Whoever it was wrote: *I got a hole in one today!*

And that was when the door opened behind me, so I had to sign out as fast as possible and pretend I was just leaving. Jess sat down beside me and I tried not to turn red.

"Are you okay, Grace?" she asked. "You look all anxious." Her eyes seemed to be searching my face for clues, but I somehow managed to smile and say I was just tired.

"What have you been doing?"

"Looking up stuff on the internet for science."

In one way it was easy to lie to Jess because she wasn't in the same science group as me and she knew I was always looking up things on the internet, so it sounded totally truthful. But in another way it was terrible lying to my best friend and I hated myself for it.

Later, when I was reading in bed but not taking in a single thing, I went over and over those messages in my mind. In the end I decided that it didn't matter whether people wanted to have private jokes or not. It was stupid of me to have gotten involved and I made a new, stricter resolution never to go in the chat room again. Then I wouldn't have to lie to Jess any more either.

Mrs. Mellor was in a great mood at the beginning of our swim team session, when we were all getting changed. She told us she'd roughly worked out who would be swimming in all the various races in the competition, and she'd definitely decide by the end of the session.

I shivered, because the weeks were flying by and the swimming competition was so near. Then, we all went back to our chatter as Mrs. Mellor went through to the pool. Felissia was wearing a different swimsuit from usual and I must have been staring, because she smiled brightly and said, "Want a photo, Grace?"

"Sorry," I mumbled. "I was just looking at your suit. It's really nice."

"Thanks." She stood in front of the mirror and started scooping her hair into a ponytail as I went through to the pool. It was true I didn't really like Felissia, because she obviously didn't particularly like me, but at least I wasn't worrying about her being the bully any more.

"Okay, girls," said Mrs. Mellor after we'd warmed up and done some free swimming, "I'd like to practice the racing dive." She reeled off twelve names, including mine and Rhianna's from Hazeldean, and she also included Felissia, Bella and Hannah. Then she sent everyone else to the shallow end to work on kick-board and pull-buoy drills, which is where you split the strokes up into different parts so you're practicing the arms and the legs separately.

Mrs. Mellor then lined us twelve up in threes behind the blocks. She put me at the front, with two girls from Elmhurst behind me. I didn't want to go first; it made me feel too much on show.

"Now, girls, during the competition I will say, 'On the blocks, please.' So front four people, do that now, please." I stepped onto the block, feeling a little nervous as though this really was the competition. "I will then say, 'Take your marks', and that is when you move to the front of the block... Yes, that's right, knees bent..." She suddenly asked everyone to look at me. "See how Grace's body is coiled, ready to explode on the starting gun..." I felt an even bigger wave of nervousness roll over me. I'd been in quite a few swimming competitions back in Thailand, but there had always been a whistle, not a gun. This suddenly seemed really official.

"Excellent, Grace. Knees bent a little more..." And just as Mrs. Mellor said that I distinctly heard a giggle from behind me, but I deliberately didn't turn around. I felt stupid standing in this position, but there was nothing I could do because Mrs. Mellor went on. "Now, this next part is when you fling your arms and body forward in order to enter the water as far down the pool as possible."

I wasn't sure whether Mrs. Mellor meant me to actually do the dive, so I just bent my knees slightly more, which meant sticking my bottom out a bit to make myself perfectly ready, and this time the giggle was so loud that I straightened back up instantly and turned around. The Elmhurst girls had turned a little pink and were trying to keep their faces straight. I glanced at the girls waiting at the next-door block. It was Felissia and her friend Cassie and they were both smirking.

"What's amusing you, girls?" Mrs. Mellor asked impatiently.

Felissia's mouth instantly stopped grinning but you could still see a mocking amusement in her eyes. At least, *I* could. Cassie was looking down. The girls from Elmhurst looked embarrassed now and everyone else just looked puzzled, even Bella and Hannah.

I demonstrated again and this time I had to actually dive in, but it wasn't my best because I definitely heard someone snicker and it threw me off. Mrs. Mellor said my dive was absolutely fine, though, which made me feel better. Still, I couldn't work out why people had been giggling. Did I look funny with my bottom sticking out? Surely we all looked the same in that position, but when the others tried it I noticed there wasn't any laughter. I tried to forget about it for the rest of the session, but didn't really succeed until the end when we were each given a pair of small flippers. It felt great going so much faster than usual and, as Mrs. Mellor said, it really did help us with our strokes.

In the changing room Evie was a bit hyper telling me about the presents she'd received at Chinese New Year, but she suddenly stopped her excited flow and I wondered what was the matter. "Look, Grace! There's a hole in the back of your swimsuit. I've just spotted it in the mirror."

I craned my neck around to look in the mirror and saw with horror that she was right. There in the middle of the bottom of my swimsuit was a definite hole. I moved to the far end of the changing room, quickly wrapped my towel around me, and pulled the suit off to have a good look. My stomach turned over as I realized it wasn't just worn out, it had been cut with a pair of scissors.

"Let's see," said Evie, coming over a moment later, but I'd already wrapped my suit up in my towel by then.

"Oh, it's nothing much," I said as lightly as I could. "I caught it on the corner of my drawer and pulled it a bit violently!" I tried to force out a giggle. "My own stupid fault. Thank goodness Katy's good at sewing!"

Evie was barely smiling. "You seem pretty relaxed about it, Grace! I'd be going nuts if that was me."

I hoped my loud heartbeat wasn't giving away how I felt. "Well, I've had this swimsuit for ages, and I've got another one, so..."

She nodded and went on toweling off her hair while I glanced across at Bella, who was keeping herself to herself and not taking any notice of anything going on around her. I looked at the girls from Elmhurst who had giggled when I was demonstrating the diving technique. I could hear them talking to two other girls from their house about entering the program design competition. My eyes moved around to Felissia, who was carefully folding her clothes, and I thought back to how she and Cassie had smirked at me. I was shivering by then.

Jess came to meet me after the practice, and we walked toward Hazeldean with Evie. I found myself tensing up, worrying that Evie might mention the hole in my suit. I knew Jess would want to see it. And then she'd be sure to insist on marching me to Miss Carol to explain about the messages and everything.

At first it was easy to keep the conversation away from swim team because Jess wasn't in the mood for talking. She'd linked her arm through mine and was strolling along, staring at the sky.

"It looks like marble with veins of steel in it, doesn't it?" she said in her soft voice.

"Why don't you get your camera and take a picture, Jess?" I asked on a burst of inspiration.

"I don't think it'd work. The light's not good enough." She suddenly seemed to snap out of her dreamy mood. "Anyway, how was swim team?"

"Great!" said Evie. "We got to wear flippers. Not those great big things – little ones that feel like an extension of your legs. It was cool, wasn't it, Grace?"

"Yeah...great! What did you do in art, Jess?"

"I worked on my entry for the swimming competition program, but I don't want to say what it is until it's finished." Jess grinned at Evie and changed the conversation back to swim team. "Flippers? You lucky things. Why don't we get to wear flippers in ordinary swimming lessons?"

"You ought to ask," said Evie.

I urgently wanted to get away from this swimming talk. "Can't I see your competition entry, Jess? I bet it's awesome."

"You can when it's finished," said Jess. Then she stopped and smiled into the distance and I thought she'd be thinking about her design, but it turned out she was picturing us all in our flippers. "I bet you were like a school of little fish gliding up and down!"

"Yes, and one fish had a hole in its swimsuit!" said Evie, pointing to the top of my head dramatically.

My heart sank as the smile dropped off Jess's face and she turned to me. "Oh no! How did that happen?"

I rolled my eyes as though I was cross with myself. "I think it was when I yanked it out of my drawer..."

"An actual hole, though?"

I nodded and shrugged. "Never mind, I've got my other suit."

"Gotta go, folks!" said Evie, turning off down the little path that led to Oakley House. "See you later!"

As soon as she'd gone, Jess wanted to see my swimsuit and wouldn't take no for an answer.

"I knew something was making you anxious, Grace," she said, as she poked her finger through the hole. "I could feel you all tense as we were walking. And no wonder." Her frown deepened. "Look, it's right in the very middle. Are you sure this happened when you pulled it out of your drawer? It looks to me like it's been cut with scissors." Her eyes softened as she turned to me. "Did everyone see it?"

I gave up trying to pretend I wasn't bothered and started explaining about the girls from Elmhurst giggling, and Felissia and Cassie smirking when I'd had to demonstrate the racing dive. "It doesn't mean it was them who did it," I quickly added. "They might have just been laughing because the hole looked funny."

Jess looked furious. "Laughing's bad enough, but I can't believe that anyone could be so nasty that they'd actually ruin someone's suit," she said in a hiss. "You've absolutely got to tell Mrs. Mellor or Miss Carol now, Grace."

"I don't want to," I blurted out. "I can't prove anything…"

"But it's not just a couple of messages any more…"

A horrible guilt swept over me. Jess would have been even more shocked if she'd known about my sweatshirt and the other messages that I'd seen in secret. My guilt mingled with big alarm. It worried me so much when there was talk of telling teachers. "But the messages might not have anything to do with this," I pointed out.

Jess wasn't listening. "I've just thought of

something," she said in a breathless voice. "Someone's actually been in our dorm. How else could they have gotten hold of your swimsuit? Do you think it was during Chinese weekend?"

I shivered, hating the conversation. The more we talked about messages and holes, the worse it all seemed. But Jess was determined to get to the bottom of it.

"Come on. Let's see what the others think."

She started to walk off, but I grabbed her arm and spoke really urgently. "No, Jess. I don't want the others to know."

"Why not?" She was looking at me as though I was crazy.

"Because they might tell...someone, thinking it's the best thing to do, even if I told them not to..."

Jess was silent, her whole expression set in a question mark, so I gabbled on, trying to convince her that it was best to keep it to ourselves. "There's no proof of who's been messaging and who's made this hole and whether it's the same person, and there's no way to find out. I don't want big announcements in assembly or anything like that. I'd feel stupid after the stuff about my stopwatch going missing. If I just ignore it all, maybe it'll just go away. Promise me you won't say anything, Jess."

A look of major alarm had come over Jess's face as I'd been talking and I had to wait for ages before she eventually nodded and sighed. "Well, if you're sure…"

"Yes, I'm certain."

"But what's going to happen next?"

"Nothing. I'll wear my spare suit and act normal. I don't want to give anyone the satisfaction of thinking they're upsetting me. I just want to find out for definite who it is who hates me so much…"

Jess suddenly looked at me with dark eyes. "It's *their* problem if they hate you, you know. And I think it's cool how sensible and strong you're being, Grace! And actually, thinking about it, sooner or later, the bully is sure to give themselves away. We just have to wait."

We walked the rest of the way to Hazeldean in silence, each in our own little worlds. *Torpedo Gal* and *Huggy Bear* were on a mission to humiliate me and stop me from swimming. Jess thought I was sensible and strong, but right now I felt sick. How could I keep pretending I wasn't bothered when inside I was hurting so much?

* * *

When it came to the swimming lesson on Friday, Katy and Naomi both asked why I wasn't wearing my other swimsuit and I just said I felt like a change. Then Katy said the turquoise color really suited me, which was nice of her.

Going through to the pool I noticed Hannah was sitting in the spectators' area, talking to Mrs. Mellor, so she'd obviously been given permission not to swim. Katy and Naomi hardly gave her a second glance, just slithered into the water, doing over-the-top gasps about how cold it was. They seemed to have completely forgotten about the "skinny loser" message that Georgie had seen. I was glad. It helped me to kid myself that everything was normal. But as I swam to the deep end, I started to feel even more uncomfortable with Hannah watching me, than when she was swimming too.

The whole lesson was devoted to backstroke. I wasn't very good at it, because I kept on going off course like Evie had done at swim practice. At one point I actually swung my arm back and hit someone by mistake.

"Oh sorry!" I said, before I'd seen who it was. "Are you all right?"

I got a shock to find it was Bella, but surprisingly she didn't look upset. "It's okay. You only hit my shoulder." I was on the point of getting ready to start swimming again when she said, "Grace...?"

"Yes." I kept my face completely straight even though I was dreading her saying something horrible.

"Nothing..."

I couldn't stop thinking about that for the rest of the lesson, wondering what Bella had been going to say. Then, as we trooped out to the changing room at the end, I heard someone ask Bella what was the matter with Hannah.

"She's not feeling well," Bella replied.

I glanced at Hannah. She was sitting very still and just kind of staring into space. I'd never seen her looking like that before. Kind of...lost. Maybe my plan was working and she'd realized her nasty bullying was having no effect at all on me, so now she didn't know what to do. I hoped I was right. It made me feel strong.

That evening I e-mailed my family and when I'd finished I tried to make myself simply leave the computer room, but my curiosity was just too great and before I knew it I'd gone into the chat room and typed in Georgie's password. *Just this once,* I promised myself. *Just this one last time.*

Immediately I took a sharp breath at the sight of the name *Torpedo Gal*. She wrote: *Hia babz. Missing you.* Then *Huggy Bear* wrote: *That's the missing link.* My heart turned over as I realized what was happening. First there were messages about holes and next thing a hole suddenly appeared in my swimsuit. Now there were messages about something missing. I felt myself trembling. That meant something was about to go missing. "Like what?" I asked the empty room.

I closed my eyes as I guessed the answer to that question. Then I opened them wide.

No, surely they wouldn't actually steal my swimsuit?

Chapter Seven

A minute later I was racing downstairs to the drying room in the basement. My whole body was shaking, and I couldn't help thinking about the time when my sweatshirt had gone missing. And now here I was again, but this time it felt worse. I was so sure I was going to find that my swimsuit had disappeared. We all hang our suits in the drying room when we don't actually want to put them into the laundry, and when I got there I rushed to the far corner where I'd left mine earlier. I nearly cried with relief to see that it was still there. It wasn't quite dry but I didn't want to take any risks, so I grabbed it quickly and went up to the dorm.

Mia was reading on the bed. I was about to put my suit in the drawer where I always keep it when I realized I had to be more careful now, so when I was sure Mia was definitely absorbed in her book, I stuffed the suit in one of my big bathrobe pockets. I was pleased with that hiding place. No one could ever think of looking for it there. Then I wondered whether it might be easier to just keep it in my school bag and walk around with it all through the day, but that wouldn't work because we have to leave our bags outside the cafeteria when we go for meals.

The next day I raced back to Hazeldean whenever I could get away from the others without drawing attention to myself. I would stick my hand inside my bathrobe pocket with a racing heart, and breathe a huge sigh of relief as my fingers touched the suit. Then on Sunday morning I decided to go swimming before breakfast. I chose that time because I was pretty sure there'd be hardly anyone there.

Jess was still half asleep in bed. "Do you want me to come with you?" she asked me in her sleep-mumble, as I call it.

"No, it's okay," I whispered. "See you at breakfast."

One thumb appeared over the quilt, so I took that as a yes.

I was right about the swimming pool being practically empty. When I first got in, there were just four eighth grade girls swimming up and down. They'd spread out and I felt like an intruder when I started swimming. They didn't say anything, just all shifted up a bit to give me most of a lane to myself. I really wanted to practice backstroke but I didn't dare in case I crashed into one of them, so I kept to front crawl and tried to breathe exactly how Mrs. Mellor had shown me. After a few lengths I felt myself get into a rhythm. There's something wonderful about swimming before breakfast. My dad and I used to do it all the time, and I always remember him saying, "Sets you up for the day, Grace, doesn't it? And the breakfast tastes ten times better afterwards!"

I think I'd done about ten lengths when Bella got into the pool and Hannah went to sit in the spectator area again, looking fed up. My spirits instantly sank and I wished I hadn't bothered to come. I'd been just starting to enjoy my training and now it was all spoiled. Surprisingly they both gave me a half smile, but I didn't give one back because I couldn't trust that the smiles were genuine. Bella got in the same lane as one of the eighth graders and started doing perfect backstroke without ever straying out of the lane. I so wished I could do that.

After a few minutes one of the eighth graders stopped swimming, then as soon as the other three finished their next length all four of them got out, breathing heavily and quietly saying, "Good job," to each other. Which just left me and Bella. I could feel her eyes on me as I continued with my front crawl. I really wanted to change to backstroke, because it was the perfect time to practice it now that the pool was so deserted, but I wasn't confident enough to do that in front of Bella.

"Grace?" I turned to see her standing up at the shallow end, her shoulders rounded as though she was cold. My heart was beating faster than usual as I looked at her and waited. "I don't suppose you could show me how to do a flip turn, could you? I can't seem to get the hang of it and I think Mrs. Mellor's getting tired of explaining it to me."

My first thought was that this was a trick, but I saw that she was sucking her lips in and looking really worried. "Um…yes…I suppose…"

I glanced at Hannah as I swam toward Bella. She was looking down at her hands in her lap.

"You…you have to try not to break the rhythm of the stroke…"

Bella nodded. I shot another quick look at Hannah, half expecting her to be smirking to herself, but she was leaning forward now with an interested look on her face.

"So you figure out which is your best arm to push yourself down into the somersault," I went on hesitantly, "and…" Bella kept nodding and frowning. I couldn't believe she was listening to me so intently. "…and be ready with that arm when you're almost at the side, but make sure you leave yourself enough turning time."

"Should I try it?" said Bella.

"Yes. I'll watch you from the side."

So I got out and sat with my knees drawn up. Bella used her left arm to push down, but I noticed she held her nose with the other hand, and I realized instantly that that was the problem.

"You see, I'm awful," she said, coming back to the surface and treading water.

"You're not," I quickly said, forgetting all about messages and holes for a moment. "It's just that you've got to try to do it without holding your nose."

She looked a little embarassed. "I know. Mrs. Mellor keeps telling me that. I tried it once, only the water went up my nose and really hurt, then afterwards I was spluttering so much I decided never to try it again."

"It'll be all right as long as you breathe out through your nose the whole time you're doing it."

She looked doubtful. "Are you sure?"

"Yes, honestly. Imagine you're trying to blow bubbles through your nose. Just do a half turn at first to get used to it."

So she did, and when she came up she looked much more confident. "Yes, you're right. It works. I'm going to try a full one now. Here goes!"

She swam from about halfway up the pool and did a perfect flip turn without holding her nose, and came up grinning like crazy. "I did it! Oh wow! I actually did it!"

I couldn't help laughing because she looked so happy, and from the spectator area Hannah broke into applause and did a whoop. Even the lifeguard looked impressed and gave Bella a thumbs up.

"Oh thank you, Grace. You ought to be a swimming instructor, you know!"

My mind was reeling as I suddenly realized that here I was having a great time with Bella and Hannah, and only a few minutes before I'd been totally scared of them. "I don't suppose you can give me any tips on how to do backstroke in a straight line, can you, Bella?"

"Well...I'll try, but I'm not sure what to tell you really. I just seem to go straight..."

Hannah stood up. "I always look at some kind of mark on the wall," she called out. "Then every four strokes I check I'm still in line with it. If you check more often than that it puts you off your stroke." She pointed to the far wall. "You could use the window frame or whatever's right opposite you when you set off."

"Oh thanks," I called back. "I'll try that."

So I did, and it worked, which got me another round of applause from Hannah and a big smile from Bella.

I was totally certain now that I had it completely wrong about these girls and I couldn't help feeling guilty. They must have thought I was really stuck-up before, because whenever they'd looked at me, I'd looked away. I wanted this friendly time to continue for longer so they could realize I was a nice person really.

"Are you still not feeling well, Hannah?" I asked. She glanced at the lifeguard, then shook her head, which I thought probably meant that she didn't want to say anything with grown-ups listening, so I swam to the spectator end and got out of the pool. "When do you think you'll be able to start swimming again?" I asked quietly.

She shrugged and looked down. Then Bella got out and raised her eyebrows at Hannah. I knew what that look was saying. It was asking Hannah if it was okay to tell me something secret.

Hannah shrugged again and Bella whispered, "The thing is, Hannah's suit has gone missing..."

My stomach yo-yoed. There it was. I saw it instantly this time. *The missing link.* Only it wasn't *my* suit that had gone missing. It was Hannah's.

"I just don't get it," said Hannah. "I put it in the laundry and when I went to get my pile of stuff, my swimsuit wasn't there. I checked with our dorm mom and she said she was sure it was there when she sorted through everything. She was going to ask around to see if one of the other girls took it by mistake, but it's obvious they wouldn't."

"Why not?"

Hannah hung her head, which made me sorry I'd asked the question. "Because no one's as big as me. All the other suits are miles smaller, so how could anyone get them mixed up?"

"Apart from me!" said Bella, grinning. "But I obviously don't have it."

My head was spinning, but not with thoughts, with emotions. I felt so sad for Hannah, but I also felt the most enormous feeling of relief and happiness. Although there was still the tiniest feeling of uncertainty. What if Hannah and Bella were incredibly good actors, and this whole conversation was fake, and they were really the bullies? No. They couldn't possibly be acting. *No one* could act this well.

I was suddenly really tempted to tell them everything about the messages and the hole in my swimsuit and the connection that I'd just made between the message with the word *missing* in it, and the fact that Hannah's suit was missing. But I tried to be sensible and not go blurting things out until I'd thought them through some more.

"So you don't have a...spare suit?" I asked carefully.

Hannah turned red but didn't reply.

I waited.

"Tell Grace..." said Bella quietly.

It took Hannah ages to speak. She seemed to be taking the biggest, slowest breath in the world.

"I don't have a spare one, no. So...I called Mom and she went nuts and said it was the school's fault my suit has gone missing, and she refused to buy a new one because she thinks the school isn't making enough effort to find out what happened to it."

Hannah bit her lip and looked down, so Bella went on with the story. "Mrs. Ansell – that's our dorm mom – asked if anyone had a spare one that Hannah could borrow...and one of the seventh graders lent her one..."

"And I tried it on..." Hannah said in scarcely more than a whisper, "...only it's too small, which is so embarrassing." I wondered if I ought to be saying something, but I couldn't think what to say. I just felt so sorry for Hannah. She seemed to be pulling the words from deep down inside her. "So...I'm like...pretending it's okay...but I've told Mrs. Ansell I can't swim because of stomach cramps, which is a lie." Hannah's voice dropped and so did her eyes. "But I can't make the stomach cramps go on and on and on, so I just...don't know what to do."

My heart was going out to Hannah. "I'm sure... your suit will turn up." I was irritated with myself for not being able to think of anything more comforting to say. I tried again. "Willowhaven would miss you like crazy if you didn't swim. You're such a strong swimmer."

"I won't stand a chance if I don't even enter," she said miserably.

"But...what does Mrs. Mellor suggest?"

"I've lied to *her* as well," Hannah said in a thin voice.

I was racking my brain for something reassuring to say, but still couldn't think of anything so I just murmured, "Oh poor you."

Bella glanced up at the clock. "We'd better go to breakfast."

"Yes...I'm really sorry about...everything, Hannah." Then I decided to check something out. "You don't think...anyone might have taken it on purpose?"

Hannah shook her head. "Why would anyone want *my* swimsuit?" She turned sadly to Bella. "I'll wait for you outside."

Bella and I were both wrapped up in our own thoughts and didn't talk at all in the changing room until we were putting our socks and shoes on.

"Hannah and I didn't used to think you liked us, Grace."

A thousand thoughts about how to reply crowded into my head as I slowly turned to face her, but none of them seemed right, so I just said, "I...didn't think you liked me either."

She looked genuinely shocked and hurt. "Why?"

"I dunno…I thought you thought I was a show-off…"

She was sitting still as a statue with one sock in her hand. "Why?"

A squirmy feeling was taking me over. I looked down. "You seemed to be watching me, kind of… disapprovingly."

"Disapprovingly?"

I nodded.

"Oh sorry, Grace, we didn't mean to stare or anything…" The words came tumbling out. "But Hannah and I always talk about you, how you're really skinny, and how we wish we looked like you, and…everything."

My heart missed a beat, but I recovered quickly. Just because she'd used the word *skinny*, it didn't mean anything. I was still double certain that Bella and Hannah were being genuine. In fact, I felt totally awful for ever suspecting them. "Sorry, I didn't realize…"

"It's okay."

When we went outside we found Hannah hovering a little distance away and Jess photographing the swimming pool window. She must have been aware of me out of the corner of her eye, but went on looking through her lens as she spoke.

"You were right, Grace. The window looked great with the sun shining on it. I could see reflections from outside and just a smudgy trace of inside, but then the sun went in when I was just about to take the photo... Never mind."

I heard the click of the shot being taken, then Jess turned to me and her mouth actually made an "o" shape when she saw who I was with. I nearly laughed, she looked so funny, but instead I went over and asked if I could look through her lens. Then as I took the camera from her I quickly whispered that I trusted Bella and Hannah now. Jess looked a little confused at first, but she seemed to accept what I'd told her and the four of us set off walking together like old friends, chatting about Jess's photography.

"Why did you want to take that picture of the pool window?" asked Bella, looking puzzled.

"It was Grace's idea actually," said Jess. "Windows are my latest thing, you see! But I'm going to come back another time and take this one again when the sun's shining and I can get the reflection of the trees." She turned and eyed the windows of Beech House in the distance, then pointed to the very top one. It was open a couple of inches and the curtains were half closed. "Windows like that one are really interesting to me. I ask myself questions, like, are there people in there? What are they doing? Do they want to get out or are they safe inside?"

"Hang on a sec," I said. "That's Felissia's dorm, isn't it?"

Hannah shrugged and made a face. "I don't like Felissia," she said firmly, "because she doesn't like me."

"H...how do you know?" I asked hesitantly.

"Just do. The way she looks at me."

"And me," said Bella quietly.

I didn't say anything, but lots of thoughts were gathering in my mind. Perhaps Felissia was the person behind everything that had happened, after all. Anyway, I was sick of all this uncertainty and worry, and poor Hannah was in a terrible state. I was suddenly filled with determination to find out who was the bully. I didn't know how on earth to go about it, but somehow I would. For Hannah's sake, and for mine.

Chapter Eight

It's usually volleyball practice after school on Mondays, but this Monday it was canceled because the volleyball coach was sick, so I decided to go swimming instead. Bella had texted me and asked if I was going swimming and she said she thought she'd come along too. She told me that Hannah didn't want to, because she was fed up with watching and not being able to join in.

"But what's she going to do when it comes to Thursday?" I squeaked when I met her outside the pool. "It's the swimming competition!"

"I know. We're both really worried about that.

I think she's just kind of hoping her suit'll turn up by some miracle."

My mind was spinning. This was terrible. I *had* to think of a way of proving it was Felissia bullying me and Hannah, and I had to do it right now, because time was running out. It gave me a shock to go through to the foyer and find that who should be standing in front of the noticeboard with Stella and Cassie but Felissia. She was stabbing her finger down the list and counting. "One, two, three, four! Huh! That's ridiculous!"

Bella rolled her eyes and scurried off into the changing room, but I stayed right where I was because of what I heard Felissia say next.

"She's in *four* races! That is *so* unfair!"

"How many is Hannah in?" asked Cassie.

"Three," said Stella. "And so is Bella."

And Felissia immediately came back, "And so am I! Mrs. Mellor must have made a mistake." Stella and Cassie stayed quiet. But Felissia hadn't finished. Her voice was cold and hard. "I bet I know what's happened. I bet Grace went sucking up to Mrs. Mellor and asked for another one. That's the kind of girl she is! One big show-off, who thinks she's so wonderful at everything she does."

My hackles rose and before I had time to think,

I blurted out, "I am *not*! How dare you make up things about me, Felissia Streeter? I never asked Mrs. Mellor anything." Then I stood there, my shoulders tense and my body shaking with a mixture of anger and a kind of fear at my own boldness.

Felissia swung around, eyes flashing. "I'm not making things up. Everyone thinks it. You train the whole time because you're obsessed with winning..."

"I do *not* train the whole time!"

I saw her flick a sneering glance at my swimming bag. "Well that's what you're just about to do now!" And with that Felissia turned and stalked straight out of the building, but not before I heard her horrible voice ringing out, "See! She didn't have an answer to that, *did* she?"

My body felt like a lead weight as I looked at the noticeboard. Before that conversation had happened, I wouldn't have minded finding out that I was the only one in sixth grade to have been picked for four races, but now I couldn't feel enthusiastic at all. I just felt shaky and afraid. Mrs. Mellor had me down for the fifty meters front crawl, the fifty meters backstroke, the medley relay and the freestyle relay. I ran my finger down the list and saw that Felissia had been picked for three of the same races.

I didn't enjoy training that day one little bit because of being so mad about Felissia. And I stayed mad for the next two days, while my determination to prove that she was the bully grew stronger and stronger, even though I hadn't managed to come up with any plan yet. But when it came to swim team my anger spilled over into a completely different feeling. You see, Hannah didn't turn up at all and Bella whispered to me that she was in bed, having to pretend that her stomach cramps had gotten much worse, and dreading admitting to Mrs. Ansell that the spare swimsuit she'd gotten from the seventh grader girl was too small.

"She was crying when I saw her at lunchtime," said Bella, "because she'll have to miss the swimming competition and she's missing lessons and everything. But she's still scared to tell the truth in case Mrs. Ansell makes her try on some other spare suits and none of them fit."

I felt so sorry for Hannah and so powerless to help. "Couldn't you just go and explain to Mrs. Ansell yourself?" I asked Bella.

"No, because Hannah's made me swear I won't." Bella was almost in tears herself by now. "She wants it kept secret, Grace. You haven't told anyone, have you?"

I shook my head.

"Promise me you won't tell."

I'd been about to say that if *I* were her, I'd go ahead and tell Mrs. Ansell anyway, but then I remembered how I'd begged Jess and the others not to tell a teacher about the chat-room messages, and how upset I would have been if they'd ignored me and told Miss Carol behind my back.

"I promise."

"I feel so helpless," said Bella.

And that was the precise moment that the perfect plan popped into my head, making me tingle all over because it was so clever.

I couldn't concentrate at all during study hour that evening, as my mind was spinning with thoughts of what I was going to do afterward. As soon as it finished, I grabbed Jess and whispered, "Got something important to tell you. Come with me."

A minute later we were in the computer room.

"What are you doing?" asked Jess, totally aghast as she watched me type in Georgie's password.

"I've done it before, it's okay."

"What!"

I didn't even turn around at the sound of her

breathless gasp. I was on a mission and nothing seemed to matter any more except getting Felissia found out. Then I'd tell Hannah, and she could tell Mrs. Ansell, and Mrs. Ansell could arrange for Felissia's dorm to be searched. She absolutely must have Hannah's swimsuit hidden away somewhere.

"The bully is definitely Felissia," I gabbled. "I'll explain how I know afterwards, but I really need your help, Jess."

Jess was silent, but she seemed totally caught up with what I was doing. Her eyes were glued to the screen. "Look!"

The name *Torpedo Gal* had come up. I leaned forward.

"*Is obsession good?*" I read out loud.

There were five other people online and, one by one, four of them replied.

No.

Course not.

Garbage.

Why?

And then I typed in my own reply. <u>Who's</u> *obsessed?*

Finally Jess spoke. "What are you doing, Grace?" she asked anxiously. "They'll think it's Georgie."

"I know. I want them to."

Jess squashed beside me on the chair. "Why?"

"So we can continue with this conversation."

"Why?"

"Because I'm going to catch Felissia."

"Look, *Torpedo Gal* has replied," said Jess in a whisper, as though *Torpedo Gal* might be able to hear us. She read the message out loud slowly. "*RACE. Sorry. I mean GRACE.*"

I felt my face flooding with color. I'd never realized how close my name is to the word "race."

You're only jealous, I wrote.

Jess stiffened beside me. "Georgie's sure to find out you've been impersonating her, you know."

"I don't think she'll mind when she finds out why. This is important. Listen, Jess…"

But there was a reply already. *Ure joking! Jealous of HER? She's a DISGrace.*

"Listen, Jess," I tried again, as I stood up. "I absolutely know it's Felissia because she actually said I was obsessed, to my face, this afternoon. She was counting up how many races I was going to be in at the swimming competition. She hates me, Jess, because I'm in more races than her, and swimming was always *her* thing. But I've still got to be totally sure it's her before I tell anyone else. Can you keep

117

on pretending to be Georgie and keep Felissia talking online?" I was at the door now.

"Where are you going?" asked Jess, with panic in her eyes.

"To Beech House." There were butterflies in my stomach, but I had to be brave. For Hannah's sake.

"It's twenty to nine. You know we're not allowed out after eight thirty!" said Jess. "Are you sure you're thinking straight, Grace?"

I nodded.

"But what should I write?"

"Put, *We've always known it was you sending pathetic messages but you don't scare Grace so you shouldn't have bothered…*" Jess's eyes were wide. She'd probably never heard me sounding so full of fight. "Yes, and you can say we also know it was her who ruined Grace's swimsuit and she's going to pay for it because we're going to tell. I just need to see her writing with my own eyes, then she won't be able to deny it. And then I *will* go and tell Miss Carol, honestly. *And* you can say that we know she took my sweatshirt too."

Jess looked totally stunned. "Is that true, Grace?"

I nodded and bit my lip. "I couldn't tell you. You would have made me go to a teacher."

"But...what if Georgie comes in and sees what I'm doing?"

I was itching to get away. If my plan was to work I had to go right now, as fast as I could, before Felissia signed out and went off to bed. But I felt sorry for Jess. I'd dragged her into the middle of a nasty drama. "Say it's my fault and I'm sorry but it was all I could do to prove it's Felissia."

The lost look on Jess's face stayed at the front of my mind all the time I was running to Beech House. An older girl was just going out of the big front door and she held it open for me, so I slipped inside and ran along the hall by the stairs. I knew exactly where the computer room was from when we'd been around all the boarding houses on Chinese New Year's Day. So far I'd only seen one person and I was almost there. My plan was working perfectly, apart from my heart thumping too loudly. I was praying that Jess had managed to keep *Torpedo Gal* talking online, as I gathered together every last drop of courage I possessed and opened the door quietly to see Felissia and Cassie hunched over the first of the computers and Stella on the one next to them. They must have been completely absorbed in what they were doing, because not one of them even seemed to realize anyone had come into the room. I crept forward on shaky legs until I was close enough to see the words Felissia was typing.

I don't care what Grace thinks. She'll never be able to prove anything.

And that was when I spoke, in the hardest voice I could manage. "Oh won't she?"

I wished that Hannah had been there to see the look of big alarm on Felissia's face when she swung around and saw me there. Her mouth fell open and the other two went white. For a split second I felt a giddy feeling of power, but then my knees nearly buckled at the sound of an icy voice behind me.

"What's going on here?" I turned to see Miss Walton, the dorm mom of Beech House. Her eyebrows were arching high, and when she saw me they went even higher. "I'm sorry, I don't know who you are, but I *do* know you're not from Beech House and as it's quarter to nine, you know perfectly well you should be in your own boarding house."

"Yes, but…" It suddenly seemed like an impossible job to try and explain that I'd had to do something wrong to make something else right.

Miss Walton put her hands on her hips and tipped her head to the side, her eyes never leaving my face. "Well?"

I caught a look of triumph in Felissia's eyes and

just knew that she would have signed out of the chat room by now.

"Felissia's been posting nasty messages about me in the chat room," I said, feeling my face flooding with color as I realized the ridiculousness of what I was saying.

"That's a total lie, Miss Walton, honestly!" said Felissia in a sugary voice, her face all innocence and shock.

I could have kicked myself for ever imagining that this whole plan was any good. It was utterly stupid, because I hadn't thought it through properly. My eyes met Felissia's and the coldness I saw there shocked me, but then a second later she turned to Miss Walton with her innocent expression back in place. "And Grace and her friends have been writing really awful things."

Miss Walton fixed me with her icy glare, and I didn't dare defend myself. I wished I could sit down, my body felt so weak. Her tone was brisk. "Which house are you in?"

"Hazeldean."

"Okay, you'd better get back there right away. I'll call Miss Carol to tell her you're on your way."

"But—"

"But nothing. I'm fed up with this silly chat room

nonsense. I've said right from the word go that it would lead to trouble and, now it has, perhaps the school might come to its senses and shut it down!"

I didn't look at Felissia again, just crept out of the room and out of Beech House. Then I jogged back to Hazeldean with leaden legs, working out what on earth I was going to say to Miss Carol. If Jess was in trouble too, I'd never be able to forgive myself for concocting such a terrible plan. Not only had it not worked, but it had made things ten times worse now Miss Walton was talking about shutting down the chat room.

Miss Carol was waiting for me at the front door. "Grace!" she said, looking horrified. "Whatever are you doing out so late? I couldn't believe it when Miss Walton called just now."

I took a deep breath. I could only repeat what I'd just said to Miss Walton, but I desperately hoped that Miss Carol might be more understanding. "Someone's been sending nasty messages about me in the chat room, and I didn't know who it was, but I had a strong idea and I just needed to prove it to myself. I couldn't think of any other way of doing it. I had to actually catch the person, you see. And... now I have."

Miss Carol looked very serious. "And who was it?"

"Felissia Streeter."

"I see." She looked down and I could tell she wasn't sure what to say. "Well, we'll talk about it tomorrow, and, in the meantime, off you go to bed." She didn't exactly smile, but she didn't look quite so upset either.

The moment I went into the dorm, Jess grabbed me. "Are you okay? What happened?"

The others were all looking at me with big curiosity and I wasn't sure how much they knew about what had been going on.

"Where have you been?" asked Georgie.

I sighed as I grabbed my washbag. "It's a long story."

Jess came with me to the bathroom and I explained in a gabble all that had happened. Then I remembered that I wasn't the only one in this horrible drama. "And what about you? Did you get discovered?"

She shook her head. "Felissia wrote some pretty horrible things, though," she said, wrinkling her nose.

"Like what?"

"Going on about obsession and stuff..."

"And what did you write back?"

"I just said she was talking trash, basically."

"Thanks, Jess," I said, giving her a hug. "Goodness knows what's going to happen now," I added quietly. "I know I've made everything a hundred times worse, but at least I've proved to myself that it's definitely Felissia." I was drying my face when I suddenly remembered the thing that Felissia had said earlier that had hurt me the most. "Jess?"

She waited.

"Do you think *everyone* thinks I'm a show-off?"

In a flash, her arm was around my shoulders. "Of course they don't! *No one* thinks you're a show-off, apart from Felissia." She looked at me carefully in the mirror. "There's more to it than that, though, isn't there, Grace?"

I fiddled with my towel and saw that her eyes were full of sympathy.

"Should we call a friendship meeting so you can tell us all what's going on?"

I almost said no, but I then realized there was no need to worry that they'd tell an adult any more, because two adults already knew so it wouldn't make any difference. And I also realized that I was tired of keeping everything to myself. I couldn't say anything about Hannah because I'd promised not to, but it would be a big relief to share my own secrets.

"Okay."

The anxious look left Jess's face immediately and I knew I'd made a good decision.

Chapter Nine

I usually wake up easily in the mornings, but the morning after our friendship meeting I felt exhausted. After Miss Fosbrook had been in to make sure our lights were out and we were all quiet, we'd gotten up and sat on the round rug talking for ages and ages.

I'd told my friends absolutely everything, except the part about Hannah, and they'd been so kind and sympathetic that I'd felt like bursting into tears quite a few times. Mia said she thought I'd been very brave to keep it all to myself and Naomi said she was sure that everything would be sorted out once I'd had a good talk with Miss Carol. But I wasn't so sure myself.

Before breakfast Miss Jennings told me in a serious voice that Miss Carol wanted to see me after lunch, so I spent the whole morning worrying about what she'd say. When I went to her room right after lunch, I even took my swimsuit with me so I could show her.

"I've spoken to Miss Walton now and she's heard Felissia's side of the story," began Miss Carol, "so I just need to hear what *you've* got to say, Grace."

It suddenly seemed very unfair that I hadn't really done anything wrong except for going out of the boarding house after eight thirty, and yet here I was, having to explain my side of the story. I took a deep breath and reminded myself how Naomi had said she was sure it would be fine once I'd explained everything. Then I started talking. I began with the first message Georgie had got, but when I said it out loud, it sounded stupid. The expression on Miss Carol's face didn't change as I told her what the other messages had said. She even kept her grave look in place when I showed her the hole in my swimsuit and explained about the messages with the word "hole" in them, and I could feel my hands getting sweaty. I was careful not to mention Hannah at all, so I finished up by saying that I'd had to actually catch Felissia typing a nasty message about me to prove that she was the bully.

"And did you catch her?" asked Miss Carol in a low voice.

My mouth felt dry. "Yes, she was writing, *I don't care what Grace thinks. She'll never be able to prove anything.*"

Miss Carol blinked in surprise. "Really! Well that's really strange, because Felissia says she wasn't writing anything at all to do with you and that she's never written anything about you in her life, and she had no idea why you rushed in on her like that."

I stared at Miss Carol in amazement and was on the verge of accusing Felissia of lying when I swallowed my words. I mustn't say anything to make things worse. "B...but what about this?" I showed her the swimsuit again. "See, it's definitely been cut."

"Yes, I agree it does look as though it's been cut, but I'll need to look at this carefully, Grace, because I'm afraid it's a big leap from your swimsuit being cut to assuming it was done by Felissia."

"But what about the messages...all about holes?"

Miss Carol licked her lips and said, "Hmm," then tapped her fingers on the table as she looked at the wall. Finally her eyes met mine again. "I'm sorry, Grace, but I think it's six of one and half a dozen of the other. This is all about two girls who are both very good swimmers and have gotten themselves carried away with a bit of silly rivalry."

"A bit of..."

"Silly rivalry," Miss Carol finished off firmly, giving me a teachery look.

I couldn't believe what I was hearing. This was exactly the reason why I'd not wanted to tell a grown-up. There still wasn't any proof. Yes, I'd proven it for myself, but that wasn't good enough. And never would be.

"You'd better go to class," said Miss Carol.

"Will the chat room be shut down?" I asked quietly.

"Miss Walton is in favor of shutting it down, but we'll have to see what other people think. I'm not stopping you or anyone else from using it at Hazeldean for the time being, but I hope that you and Felissia have both learned a lesson from all this."

The others were waiting for me outside Miss Carol's room and as we walked across to our next class I told them what she'd said.

Georgie was furious. "She ought to have seen some of those messages," she snapped, "then she'd soon realize that's it's not six of one and half a dozen of the other, it's a dozen of one and zippo of the other!"

I couldn't even raise a smile at Georgie's wit. In fact, at that moment, I thought I might never smile again, I was so depressed. There didn't seem any point in anything. When I was little and Mom said I had to go to bed, I often used to stomp my foot and say, "It's not fair!" But that's a thing that all kids say. This was different. This really wasn't fair, because Hannah and I were being bullied and no one was putting a stop to it. Thinking of Mom made me suddenly homesick and that depressed me even more. Everything seemed pointless. Why should I bother to try and get better at swimming? If I won my races, Felissia would take it out on me even more, and if I didn't win them because I hadn't tried my hardest, I'd be letting down my house and myself. So I couldn't win either way.

"I'm not going to swim team," I told Jess on Wednesday after school.

Jess gasped. "You can't just not go," she said. "What are you going to tell Mrs. Mellor? It's the swimming competition tomorrow. This is your last chance to practice!"

"I'll say I'm not well," I said flatly.

"But Mrs. Mellor will check it out with Miss Carol."

I shrugged. I knew I wasn't being myself but I couldn't help it. Nothing mattered any more. "I don't care."

Jess didn't seem to know what to do. She hovered around me for a few seconds, then said, "I'd better go to art club... I'll...see you later."

I saw Bella heading toward the pool and asked her to tell Mrs. Mellor that I wasn't well.

"Oh no!" said Bella, looking devastated. "What's the matter with you? Please don't say *you* won't be in the swimming competition either!"

I shrugged, "Dunno," and started to walk off, but Bella stopped me.

"What's the matter?" she asked sternly. "Something's really wrong, I can tell. You're not acting normal."

I closed my eyes, then opened them slowly, wondering if I could be bothered to tell the whole horrible story again. In the end I sighed and just gave her the bare facts in a flat blah-blah voice, about the messages and how they connected to things which had actually happened. Bella's eyes widened when I said the words *missing link,* and *I'm missing you.* Her hand flew to her mouth. "Oh no, and Hannah's suit went missing!" she murmured, looking pale. I didn't say anything to that, but just finished off with how I'd wanted to prove to myself that it was definitely Felissia and then it would all have been done. "Only it didn't exactly work out like that," I said heavily, "because even though I proved it to *myself*, it doesn't actually prove a thing to the teachers, and anyway Felissia is basically saying she doesn't know what I'm talking about, so that's the end of that."

Bella stayed still as a statue for a few seconds, then suddenly put her hand on my arm and gave me an urgent look. "Did you tell anyone the part about why you thought Hannah's suit had gone missing?"

I shook my head. "You told me not to mention it, so I didn't."

"Okay! See you later!" And with that she was gone, so I turned and trudged slowly back to Hazeldean, wondering if there really was something wrong with me, I had so little energy.

The rest of that day was a bit of a blur. My brain seemed to shut down and my body ached. I went straight to bed, and when Jess got back from art club she got Miss Jennings to see me. Then Miss Carol came along too. I had my temperature taken twice and they both asked me lots of questions about what exactly was the matter with me, but I didn't even have the energy to speak, and I could feel my eyes balancing tears that I knew would drop onto my cheeks if I dared to blink, so I turned away and let them roll onto the pillow.

It was only six o'clock but I was already sliding into sleep, dreaming that I was locked in the swimming pool building and all the teachers were saying that unless I got in the pool and swam sixty lengths right away I wouldn't be allowed out. It was a relief to wake up after that nightmare, but in no time at all I found myself in another dream where I was locked out of the swimming pool building, banging on the door and screaming, "Let me in!" But Felissia was behind the door, laughing and pointing at me, saying, "No Grace! No race!" over and over again.

Sometime later Jess leaned over me and whispered, "Night, Grace."

I managed to say "Night" back and she told me in her gentlest voice that I didn't have to worry because Miss Carol was sorting everything out. And then Miss Carol was patting my arm and saying, "Sleep well. You'll feel better in the morning." So then I dreamed that Miss Carol was going around the whole school looking for Hannah's suit, but she never found it.

It was dark when I next woke up. By the light of my little bedside lamp I saw that my watch said six thirty-five. I felt wide awake, and it was no wonder because I'd been asleep for ages. I sat up in bed and thought about everything that had happened the day before. I also remembered with a shock that this was the day of the swimming competition. I was expecting to feel depressed, but in fact I felt fine and couldn't figure out why that was. Then I remembered what Jess had said to me about Miss Carol sorting everything out. I was desperate to wake Jess up and ask what exactly she meant by that, but it would be cruel to cut off her sleep when she had another twenty-five minutes to go.

I got up to go to the bathroom, noticing that the lead weights seemed to have left my legs and my whole body felt lighter. On the way back I saw Miss Jennings coming out of her room. She asked me how I was feeling and I said I thought I was all right, but I couldn't tell for sure yet. She nodded and said, "Good!" Then her eyes lit up. "We want our best swimmers in good shape today."

When I got back to the dorm, Naomi and Mia were both sitting up in bed, and Jess woke up a moment later at the sound of Naomi's voice asking me how I was feeling.

"Guess what!" said Jess as soon as she saw me. Then she tumbled into the fastest gabble I'd ever heard her use. "Bella told Hannah what you said about Felissia and everything, and Hannah went straight to Mrs. Ansell. We all met up at dinner and Bella told us Mrs. Ansell's lent Hannah her own swimsuit and Hannah's over the moon because it's a really trendy one. And Mrs. Ansell came to see Miss Carol during study hour – we saw them saying bye to each other when we came out at the end. So then I asked to see Miss Carol and I went nuts and said it wasn't fair that no one believed you about Felissia and now you were sick because you were so upset. And Miss Carol said I wasn't to worry any more because it had all been sorted out, and I said that I didn't care about *me* worrying, I only cared about *you* worrying, so that's why she came to see you last night..." Jess suddenly stopped talking and looked at me carefully. "You do remember her coming in when you were half asleep, don't you?"

I nodded but couldn't reply because she was rattling away again, and I noticed that Georgie and Katy were wide awake and tuning in too. "Anyway, this is the best part, because Georgie went to the bathroom during study hour and she actually heard Miss Carol and Mrs. Ansell talking, so she stayed out of sight around the corner and listened in!"

"Let me tell her this part!" said Georgie, who looked as though she was bursting.

Jess's eyes gleamed. "Go on, then. Quick! I can't wait for Grace to hear this!"

"Drum roll!" said Georgie. She grinned at me.

The excitement in the dorm was infectious. I couldn't wait to hear what was coming.

"We-ell…" Georgie went on slowly and dramatically, emphasizing all the names, "Mrs. *Ansell* told Miss *Carol* that Mrs. *Mellor* had been to see her about Hannah's swimsuit, because Mrs. Mellor found it!"

"Where?" I gasped.

Georgie looked over-the-top mysterious and I knew she was loving spinning out the tale, but I was wishing she'd get on with it now. "In Felissia's hands!"

"What?"

"Apparently Mrs. Mellor was in that little storeroom at the other end of the pool and she happened to see Felissia come creeping into the pool, fully dressed and carrying something black, so she watched and she saw Felissia furtively make for the spectators' area and put the black thing down in the farthest corner under a seat. Then, fast as anything, Felissia rushed out of the pool area and out of the whole building. So then Mrs. Mellor went straight over and found that the black thing was a swimsuit, and she asked around and discovered that Hannah had lost her swimsuit, so she went to see Mrs. Ansell, and then Mrs. *Ansell* went to see Miss *Walton* and hey presto! Felissia's been caught red-handed!"

I gasped, then sighed. "That's good – for Hannah – but I still wish there was a way of proving I didn't just make up the chat-room stuff."

"Aha! There *is*!" said Jess, giving me a tight hug. "You see, Bella told us that Evie was really quiet at swim team, and she admitted to Bella that she was one of the people online when Felissia wrote that you were a *dis*grace and that you'd never be able to prove it was her saying stuff about you. And Evie knows Felissia's username. She said she'd wanted to tell a teacher but she was too scared of what might happen if Felissia found out it was her. But Bella persuaded Evie to tell Mrs. Mellor and Mrs. Mellor promised not to mention any names when she reported it to Miss Carol and Miss Walton."

I took a deep breath and let it out. "The truth. At last."

The others were all nodding vigorously.

"And the most important thing," said Katy with a twinkle in her eye, "is that Felissia's not allowed to swim in the competition! Which means Hazeldean is in with a much better chance!"

It was as though the mixed-up mess that was my life yesterday had been completely untangled and straightened out, and my world sparkled with happiness and relief. In fact, for the first time ever, I found myself actually looking forward to the competition.

Chapter Ten

The adrenaline pumped around my body as I walked with the rest of the competitors from the changing room into the pool arena. A wall of noise hit us from the spectators' area. All the girls from sixth, seventh and eighth grade who weren't swimming in the competition sat squashed up on the tiered benches, their excited chatter ringing around the pool and zinging off the walls. Even the teachers and house staff in the second row looked excited. The seventh and eighth grade competitors went to sit in the front row of the spectators' area with their towels around them, while we sixth grade competitors filed neatly into the rows of plastic chairs which had been put along each side of the pool. As soon as I was sitting down, I looked over to try and spot Jess and the others. It wasn't hard. They were jumping up and down, giving me big two-armed waves. My glance skimmed over the rest of the sixth graders and I saw Felissia, shoulders hunched and looking sulky, a couple of rows in front. No one was talking to her and she happened to glance up. Our eyes met, but she dropped her gaze instantly. It was weird. I almost felt sorry for her at that moment.

At precisely two thirty, Mrs. Mellor blew her whistle three times and there was instant silence.

"Good afternoon!" she began, and for some reason everyone burst into applause. "This year's swimming competition promises to be a hugely exciting event and I know you're all dying for the action to begin. But first, Ms. Carmichael has something to say!"

There was another burst of applause, peppered with cheering, as the principal came down from the spectators' benches to the side of the pool. I saw Jess bite her lip and I knew she was feeling that mixture of excitement and nervousness that I was feeling myself, because Ms. Carmichael was about to announce the winner of the program design. I had no idea what Jess's design was, because she'd kept it a secret, even from her friends. I crossed my fingers on both hands and tried to catch Jess's eye, but she was looking down.

"Ladies and gentlemen of the staff," said Ms. Carmichael, in her most principal-y voice, "would you kindly raise your programs to reveal the picture on the front cover..." The thunderous applause spread like wildfire from the competitors around the pool, who saw the programs first, to the rest of the spectators, as the teachers slowly turned to hold up the program for everyone to see. "Jessica Roud of Hazeldean has produced the winning design. Very well done to you, Jessica!"

Mia and Katy, who were on either side of Jess, gave her a huge hug, and then Mrs. Mellor gave Jess a signal to go down and shake hands with Ms. Carmichael. On the way she looked across at me and gave me a double thumbs up, which made everyone laugh. I was wishing I could see the picture a little more clearly but it was just too far away to make out what it was, so I'd have to wait till afterward to look at it better.

At precisely two forty I stood on my starting block, waiting. The sixth grade fifty meters front crawl was the very first race. On the starting block to my right stood Hannah, wearing Mrs. Ansell's swimsuit. Bella had told us in the changing room earlier that although Mrs. Ansell had only lent it to Hannah at first, she thought Hannah looked so much better in it than she did herself that she wanted Hannah to keep it.

I glanced nervously at Hannah and she made a face, as if to say, *Are you as scared as I am?* Then we both snapped back to staring straight ahead and getting into position, as Mrs. Mellor's voice echoed into the silence. "Take your marks..." At the stark sound of the starter gun my nervousness vanished completely and as I dived I felt my competitive spirit flooding in. There were six of us doing front crawl as hard as we could, and for a while I couldn't see any of the others at all, as I was concentrating so hard on driving myself forward. The screams of the supporters rose above the splash of the water and gave me a new strength as we forged our way along the lanes. I managed a perfect flip turn, overtaking Evie and three of the others. There was just me and Hannah in the lead and we stayed exactly level all the way down the second length, stroke after stroke after exhausting stroke. Then, just when I thought I'd die if I had to do another single one, I touched the side and heard the sound of the whistle. A single whistle. I looked to my right. Hannah lifted her goggles and her eyes danced. "We drew!" she said reaching out to give me a hug. And I thought how different this was from that other time we'd drawn, when I'd been too eaten up with worry even to smile, and Hannah had looked away, convinced I didn't like her.

"I think Hazeldean is winning!" said Georgie, jumping up and down on the benches when I went to join my friends after my last race. "Thank goodness we've got you in our house, Grace!"

I'd come level first in the front crawl, and second in the backstroke, and I'd managed to pull my team into first place for both the medley and the freestyle relays, but after a while it's impossible to keep score when there are six houses all competing. After the sixth grade, it was the seventh, then eighth grade races, and as time went on we completely lost track of the score, except it was obvious that Beech House was way behind. I expect they were all fed up with Felissia. From where I was sitting I could see her, with Cassie and Stella on either side of her as usual, but they were talking to the people in front while Felissia stared into space. I couldn't imagine what was going through her head.

"It's time!" squeaked Naomi from just behind us. "Look, Mrs. Mellor's about to announce the results."

The shouts of excitement left their blurred echoes hanging in the air, then a complete hush took over as Mrs. Mellor was joined by Ms. Carmichael and Mrs. Andrews, the vice-principal.

"Well done, girls!" came Ms. Carmichael's clear voice over the PA system. "I never knew we had such talented swimmers here at Silver Spires!" A big cheer went up. Ms. Carmichael smiled as she waited for it to die down. "Talent is twofold," she went on slowly, her eyes moving around the whole spectators' area. "It comes from within, but then it has to be coaxed out. I think we are the luckiest school in the country to have Mrs. Mellor to do that coaxing. Don't you?" We all broke into applause again and lots of people whistled. Mrs. Mellor looked really happy and blew a kiss over to the spectators' benches where we were all sitting. "So now to the scores…" The silence was gripping. Georgie clutched hold of Mia and I saw Bella do the same to Hannah just along from us. "In sixth place, Beech House." Everyone clapped and a few people groaned. "In joint fourth place, Forest Ash and Oakley." The clapping was shorter this time. "In third place,

Elmhurst." No one moved a muscle. "In second place…" Ms. Carmichael deliberately left the longest pause under the sun. When she finally said, "… Hazeldean!" the whole place erupted, and all the Willowhaven students got up and clapped high above their heads, chanting, "We are the winners!" over and over again. Ms. Carmichael, Mrs. Andrews and Mrs. Mellor were laughing away together, waiting for the place to settle down. I gave Hannah a big thumbs up when her housemates finally stopped patting her on the back, and she looked as though she was going to burst with happiness.

"Good for Willowhaven!" I whispered to Jess. And inside I felt completely calm and contented. It was strange, but I was only a little disappointed that Hazeldean hadn't won. I knew I'd done my personal best and that gave me the most amazing feeling.

Later, when we were all changed, we took a closer look at the design that had won Jess the prize. It was such a fabulous photo she'd taken of the pool window. Mrs. Mellor had stuck programs up all over the walls of the foyer and loads of older students were admiring Jess's work.

"It's so effective the way it reflects the outside

with all the trees and everything, and yet you can see inside too," said a girl named Tabitha.

"Oh yes! If you look really carefully you can actually see someone there at the very back of the spectators' area!" said another eighth grader. "But it looks like she's lost in the woods, doesn't it, because of the reflection of all the trees from outside?"

A girl from Beech House peered closely at the picture. "That's Felissia Streeter, isn't it? What's she doing there?"

Then they all wandered off, leaving just me and my friends. We looked at each other with big eyes.

"Did you realize you'd photographed Felissia?" I asked quietly.

"No, not till I saw the picture blown up on the computer screen. That was what made me decide to use it for the competition. It was just a moment in time, but to me it captured the whole feeling about the swimming competition."

Naomi peered at Jess's picture. "And what that girl said just then is so true. The way the trees are reflected in the photo, it really does look as though Felissia is lost in the woods."

Jess nodded. "And in a way, she was," she whispered so only I could hear her, and the two of us exchanged our special look which said, *Let's talk about it later*. And I knew we'd spend ages discussing that big pool window and whether it was keeping someone in or keeping someone out, and whether we ought to feel sorry for Felissia because maybe everything she'd done had come out of feeling lost.

Katy suddenly looked around furtively as though making sure that no one would hear her, then she said something that had never occurred to me. "Maybe you captured the moment of proof, Jess."

Georgie frowned. "What moment of proof?"

"Felissia hiding Hannah's suit," whispered Mia.

"Maybe I did," said Jess, with that faraway look in her eyes.

A thoughtful silence closed in around us for a few seconds until Jess's phone started to ring. She answered it quickly. "Oh hi, Mom!" Then we all drifted outside, but as Georgie chose that moment to jump up and down shouting, "Hazeldean forever!" I didn't hear anything more of what Jess was saying.

A moment later she hung up and turned to me with bright eyes. "Guess what! Mom's got two days off work at the end of spring break, and Jan and Mom have been on the phone with each other, and they've sorted out that we're spending from Saturday to Wednesday at Jan's and then Thursday to Sunday at my house!"

"What? Together? At spring break you mean?" I asked, being a little slow for a moment.

"Of course, together!" said Jess, giving me a hug. Then she linked her arm through mine and we set off back to Hazeldean. Jess was staring all around her but I wasn't looking at anything because my mind was swirling with thoughts about all that had happened.

"You're very quiet, Grace," said Jess hesitantly after a few minutes. "You do want to spend spring break together, don't you?"

"Of course I do!" I assured her. "Can't wait, in fact!"

"You're not sad because of Hazeldean not winning, are you?"

I smiled and shook my head. "No," I said, standing quite still, "I'm not sad at all because I did my personal best. I'm just thinking back over all that's happened."

"I've been thinking too," Jess said. "And I've decided something, and this is it: with all you've come through, *you* are the overall winner at Silver Spires." There was a long silent moment while Jess looked right into my eyes, in one of her little Jess-dreams. "I wish I had my camera right now," she said finally, "so I could take your photo and put it up on your board with a big heading – THE OVERALL WINNER. Then you'd never forget it."

"Don't worry," I said quietly. "I won't *ever* forget it."

School Friends Fun!

One of the best things about being at Silver Spires is the chance to spend time playing different sports and games with my friends. When I'm competing I'm deadly serious, but now you're going to see that I've got a fun side too!

 ## How to get active!

Not everyone likes the idea of serious competitive sports (including most of my friends!), but there are lots of fun games you can play instead. Some are so silly, they're bound to get you laughing as well as moving! So why not get out there and try something new? Here are a few ideas to get you started…

★ The cereal box game is great for stretching – and giving you the giggles! Place an empty cereal box upright on the ground, and each take a turn to lean over and pick it up, using only your mouth and without bending your legs. Then rip off the top part of the box so it's shorter and all have another turn…then rip off another chunk, and so on. See how low you can go without falling over!

★ Have a piggyback relay race! Split into even numbered teams and decide where you're racing to. On "go!" the first pairs should piggyback to that point, then switch so that the person carrying is carried on the way back. When you are carried, no part of your body can touch the ground – otherwise you start your turn again. Don't forget to tag the next pair! On your marks...

★ If you don't mind getting messy or wearing old clothes, play silly-string tag – it's so much fun! It's just the same as normal tag, except that whoever is "it" is armed with a can of silly string (which you can buy in party supply stores). They must hit you with the silly string in order for you to be "it," and then they pass the can to you. It's great to play at parties too!

So what are you waiting for? Grab your friends and have some School Friends fun!

Grace x

Turn the page

for a sneak preview of the next

unmissable *School Friends* story...

Princess
at
Silver
Spires

Chapter One

It's so peaceful here in the secret garden. I can sit on this bench and just think my own thoughts in silence. Not that I don't love the busy, buzzy side of boarding-school life, hanging out with my close friends in our dormitory, or at lunch, or racing around the track. But out of the six of us I think I'm the one who most needs to be alone sometimes. I came across the garden last September when I'd first started at this school. My best friend, Katy, found out about it too, and then a little later we told our other close friends where it was. It's tucked away behind a high hedge way on the other side of the athletics field and we six from Amethyst dorm think we're still the only ones who know about it.

The school is called Silver Spires, and it's the best boarding school in the world. On a day like today, when the sun shines on the main building's tall spires, they really seem to sparkle like silver. It gives me a nice warm feeling, seeing them reaching into the sky, and I love the thought that this is the same sun that shines onto my home country in Africa.

I come from Ghana, and I'm a princess, but I absolutely hate people knowing that. I tried like crazy to keep it a secret when I first came here, but in no time at all people found out, and it was exactly as I'd feared. Lots of people suddenly wanted to be my friend, not because they liked me but because they liked the idea of having a princess for a friend. But, worse than that, the ones who didn't rush to be my best friend went around saying I was stuck-up and that I thought I was something special. I was miserable for a while and it was Katy who came to my rescue. At her old school everyone had wanted to be her friend too, because they knew that her mom is a famous actress. But that's one secret that will never *ever* come out here at Silver Spires. Katy only told me about it at first, but then before fall break she told the others too. The six of us best friends from Amethyst dorm are sworn to secrecy about that now.

The glinting sun in this warm spring air is like a dim reminder of the bright sun that bakes the earth of Ghana, and I can't stop my thoughts from slipping away to all the poor people I saw last week during spring break, when I went with my family to visit our home country. It made me sad and upset when I met a girl named Abina and saw with my own eyes what she has to do every day. She's twelve years old, the same age as me, and at five o'clock each morning she goes to a muddy waterhole, where animals drink, to collect water for her family. It takes hours for the water to seep through the ground and for the mud to settle, and even then it's dirty and not safe to drink. But I visited other villages in north Ghana where a charity called Just Water has built wells and installed hand pumps, so the people there can have clean water.

My father is the president of Just Water and now I've started to help the charity too. I'm really pleased to do this work because I feel so lucky to have the life I have, when there are so many people in northern Ghana who don't even survive to my age. How can that be fair? I repeat this question over and over like a mantra to myself, sitting here alone in the fresh spring air. But I never come up with any answers, just resolutions never to forget the people of Ghana.

I shivered as I looked at my watch, and got a shock because it was six thirty. I only had a few minutes to shake off African Princess Naomi and get myself back into regular-sixth-grade-Silver-Spires Naomi, having dinner with her friends. Well, to tell the truth I never completely shake the princess part of me away, but I always try my best to keep it well hidden.

As I got closer to our boarding house, Hazeldean, I saw Katy standing outside, her shoulders hunched up and her arms folded tightly. She waved when she saw me and came running over.

I hugged her. "You look frozen, Kates!"

"So do you!"

We laughed and I realized she was right. "I've been wrapped up in my thoughts in the secret garden, but I can't say they kept out the cold very well!"

"I guessed you'd be there," said Katy, looking suddenly serious. "Are you okay?"

I knew why she was asking me that. She'd listened in complete silence yesterday evening when I'd told her all about my time in Ghana, and at the end she'd said she felt guilty that I'd spent my spring break working for a charity while she'd been having a great time in LA with her mom. "You make me feel really spoiled, Naomi," were her precise words. But I'd quickly told her not to be silly, because Katy and her mom are so close and don't get to spend much time together. Anyway, I felt ten times more spoiled than that when I saw Abina's school, which was scarcely more than a tree and a wooden hut, and I compared it with Silver Spires.

"I can't stop thinking about Abina," I told her quietly, as we walked across to the cafeteria, which is in the main building.

"You can't do any more than you're doing, working for Just Water," Katy said, linking arms with me.

Maybe she was right, but it didn't stop a little niggling voice telling me I must do more.

"Slow down, you two!" came Georgie's urgent cry from way behind. Katy and I turned around to see her half walking, half jogging, as though she was on her last legs at the end of a torturous marathon. "Why do people move so fast around here?"

I couldn't help smiling as we waited for her to catch up to us. Georgie is always so dramatic, but in a great way.

"I lost track of the time watching my *Ugly Betty* DVD," she informed us in her puffed-out voice, when she finally drew level. "It's totally cool. You should see it. I'm starving now, though. What's on the menu, do you know?"

"No clue," said Katy as I slipped back into my other world for a moment. But I quickly shook the thoughts of poverty and starvation away. I knew they didn't do anyone any good.

Georgie's best friend, Mia, was in the line for food, and beckoned to us all to join her, but I didn't think it was fair for the three of us to cut in like that, so just Georgie went ahead. A moment later she was right back, full of something she was dying to tell us. "Mia says that one of the tenth graders has been looking for you, Naomi!"

I frowned and wondered what that was about. "Did Mia say who?"

"Someone named Elise. I think she's that one with the hair like Rachel from *Friends*, but Mia said she couldn't really remember what her hair was like, just that she seemed a bit put out that you weren't around, and even more put out when Mia said she had no idea where you were." Georgie winked at us and added, "Yeah, right!" All my friends knew that if I wasn't around then I was probably in the secret garden, and they'd never let on about it. Then she looked thoughtful. "Actually I don't think it *could* have been Elise, because she's got a reputation for never deigning to speak to anyone below ninth grade!"

A few minutes later I was sitting at a table with Katy, Georgie and Mia, listening to Georgie questioning Mia on what "the girl" looked like.

"You're so funny, Georgie!" said Mia. "Totally desperate to know, when Naomi's not particularly bothered."

Georgie didn't seem to hear her. "The thing is, if it *was* Elise, it must have been something pretty important." She was getting impatient. "Come on, folks, what do you think?"

I shrugged and changed the subject, because I'd suddenly realized I hadn't seen Grace and Jess since the last class. "Where are the other two?"

"There!" said Georgie, nodding toward the door and looking quite impressed with herself, as though she'd personally magicked them up for my pleasure.

I grinned at her, and Katy and I squished up on the bench to make room for them.

"One of the tenth graders was looking for you," said Grace, as she sat down.

"Whoa! Sounding urgent now! *Quelle intrigue!*"

said Georgie, putting on a French accent.

"Who was it?" Katy asked.

"A girl named Elise," Grace replied.

Georgie gasped. "That one who looks like Rachel from *Friends*?"

Grace wrinkled her nose. "Um…does she?" Grace is the least into looks and fashion out of all of us. Her passion is sports, and when she's not in her school uniform she's in her tracksuit.

It was Jess who answered Georgie's question. "Yes, she's got streaky blonde hair and always wears a big barrette holding half of it back. And she's got a long neck and wide shoulders, and wears quite a bit of makeup," she added, which made us all laugh, it was such unexpected detail.

"What's funny about that?" asked Jess.

"Nothing!" said Grace, sticking up for her best friend. "We're all just jealous of your artist's eye that picks up every little thing."

"Did she say what she wanted?" asked Katy.

"It was right after school when we saw her and she didn't seem too pleased that she might have to wait till dinner before she saw Naomi," Grace said. Then she lowered her voice as she turned to me. "Don't worry, we didn't tell her where she could find you."

"Even though I imagine she would have paid us

for the info," Jess added. "She looked so…so anxious to get hold of you."

"Wow!" said Georgie. "I'd better be there when she *does* track you down!"

"Looks like your wish has come true," said Mia quietly.

We all followed her gaze and saw a much older student marching purposefully in our direction.

"That's her!" hissed Georgie. "That's Elise!"

I don't know why, but I suddenly felt uneasy. I hate being the center of attention and I found myself crossing my fingers that everyone was mistaken, and Elise wanted to speak to someone else. Anyone but me.

She squatted down in between Georgie and me, and Georgie immediately swizzled around a bit and leaned forward. The others were all silent too, as though waiting for a show to begin.

Elise blinked and I saw how thick her mascara was. She looked annoyed about everyone tuning in. "Uh…when you've finished, Naomi, I'd like a word," she said.

I wanted to get whatever it was over with, so I started to get up. "I'm finished *now*."

"Are you sure?" She was eyeing my half-eaten cheesecake, but there was no way I could manage it.

I was just too nervous.

I followed her out of the cafeteria, certain the others were all staring after me, and as soon as we were in the hallway she turned into an empty classroom and shut the door. She perched on a desk while I stood opposite her. Now I was really nervous. Her face was so serious I began to wonder if I'd done something terribly wrong and was about to get a big telling-off.

"Naomi…" She suddenly broke into a huge smile, then leaned forward and grabbed both my wrists dramatically. "I've got something to ask you. I know you're going to find it totally unusual and you might wonder if I've got a screw loose or something, but believe me, I *do* know what I'm doing." She nodded slowly and paused, her eyes sparkling as she looked straight into mine. "I'd like *you*…" Another pause. I wished she'd just finish her sentence. "…to be one of my two models for the fashion show before the Easter vacation!"

I didn't understand what she meant. Katy is totally into fashion and wants to be a designer when she's older, so I did know that there was going to be a fashion show. But I was certain Katy had said it was for fashion design students, because I could remember her saying she couldn't wait until she was in ninth grade so she could take part. Then I suddenly had a thought. Maybe Elise had somehow gotten to hear about the incredible hip wraps and bracelets that Katy made for all of us just before spring break for Chinese New Year, and she thought I was the one who'd done them.

"Oh, I think you might be confusing me with Katy. She's a fantastic designer."

Elise's eyes shot wide open and she dropped my wrists as dramatically as she had grabbed them. "It's nothing to do with design. *I'm* the designer. I'm saying I want you to model for me." She suddenly frowned. "You *are* Naomi Okanta, aren't you?"

I felt myself tensing up, but I wasn't sure why.

"Yes," I replied, a bit abruptly.

She looked startled and I suddenly felt like an impertinent little girl talking back to a teacher, even though she was only a tenth grader. I think I must have sounded really rude. "But...I'm only in sixth grade..."

She suddenly smiled at me as though I was a little too young to get the hang of things, and then she spoke slowly and deliberately. "Okay, Naomi, the fashion show is for the students taking fashion design this year, and yes, it's true that most of them have chosen their models from ninth and tenth grade. But..." She opened her eyes wide, then broke into an even bigger smile. "...there's nothing in the rules to say that you can't have a model from any year! And let's get one thing straight, I *didn't* choose you because you're a princess. No way."

I still felt uncomfortable though. What other reason could there be for choosing a sixth grade, except that I was pretty tall? And if she particularly wanted a black model, there were plenty of other black girls higher up the school.

"I...I don't get why you want me...?"

She tipped her head to the side and smiled even more. "Because you've got the most wonderful posture. You stand so straight and walk so smoothly. You're tall and slim and elegant..." She giggled. "Need I say more?"

I couldn't help feeling flattered by what Elise had said, but I still thought there were plenty of other girls who could do it better than me.

"I'm not sure..."

I thought I saw a tiny flash of annoyance cross her face. Maybe I should be jumping at the chance. I knew Katy would. But that's only because fashion is totally Katy's scene. Georgie would grasp the opportunity with both hands too, because she absolutely loves performing. I think the others would probably be like me, though – a little scared of the unknown.

Elise paused thoughtfully before she said her next words. "It's a big charity event, you know, Naomi."

My ears pricked up. "Oh, I didn't realize that. What charity is it?"

"Um...it's not completely been decided yet. I told Miss Owen – she's the design teacher who's in charge of the whole thing – that I thought it should be a Third World charity."

I found myself getting really interested now, as a picture of Abina flashed through my mind. "So when will it be decided?"

Elise was looking at me carefully. "Well, the thing is, Miss Owen is open to suggestions. Do you...have a preference?"

"Yes, Just Water for Ghana!" I blurted out. "That's an amazing charity. Only forty-four percent of—"

"Okay! Just Water...right..." Elise jumped up. "I'll suggest it to Miss Owen. She's been asking for specific ideas." She touched my arm. "So...are you saying yes to being my number one model?"

"I... I..." My head was swimming with doubts. I hate being the center of attention. And I'd be terrified being the only sixth grader among a bunch of ninth and tenth graders. But if I could do anything to help Just Water, then I should.

Elise must have seen the struggle I was having. "Don't worry, Naomi. Think about it for a couple of days and I'll talk to Miss Owen about whether we can choose your charity...what was it? Just Water?"

I nodded.

"I'll get her to look it up on the internet. Then I'll come and find you tomorrow and you can tell me then, all right?"

I nodded weakly and she was gone like a whirlwind, leaving me in a strange daze, still flattered to have been asked and excited at the thought that I might be able to do something for my beloved charity, but confused and uneasy, and not really sure why.

To find out what happens next, read

Princess
at
Silver
Spires

Secrets, hopes and dreams...

School Friends

are forever!

Welcome to Silver Spires

Katy is nervous about going to boarding school for the first time, especially as she's got a big secret to hide. The girls in her dorm seem really nice, but when someone sets Katy up, how will her new friends react?

Drama at Silver Spires

Georgie loves acting and is determined to win her favorite role in the school play. But her audition goes wrong and an older girl steals the show instead. Will Georgie ever get her chance in the spotlight now?

Rivalry at Silver Spires

Grace is at Silver Spires on a sports scholarship and feels the pressure to do well in competitions. But when someone starts writing hurtful messages saying she's a show-off, she loses her nerve. Can she still come out on top?

Princess at Silver Spires

Naomi hates the attention that comes with people knowing she's a princess. But when she's asked to model in a fashion show, she can't refuse – after all, it's for her favorite charity. What could go wrong?

Secrets at Silver Spires

Jess is really struggling with her classes. She can't ask her friends for help, because she doesn't want them to find out she isn't as smart as them. But now that she's being made to go to special classes, how long can she keep her secret to herself?

Star of Silver Spires

Mia's ambition is to be a real musician. She'd love to enter a song she's written in the Silver Spires Star contest, but then she'd have to play live onstage too. And performing in public is her biggest fear ever – can she find the courage to overcome it?

Ann Bryant's School Days

Who was your favorite teacher?

I had two. Mr. Perks – or Perksy as we called him –
because when I was only eleven, he let me work on
a play I was writing during class! When I was older,
my favorite teacher was Mrs. Rowe, simply because
I loved her subject (French) and she was so young
and pretty and slim and chic and it was great seeing
what new clothes she'd be wearing.

What were your best and worst classes?

My brain doesn't process history, geography or
science and I hated cooking, so those were my least
favorite subjects. But I was good at English, music,
French and PE, so I loved those. I also enjoyed art,
although I wasn't very good at it!

What was your school uniform like?

We had to wear a white shirt with a navy blue tie
and sweater, and a navy skirt, but there was actually
a wide variety of styles allowed – I was a very small

person and liked pencil-thin skirts. We all rolled them over and over at the waist!

Did you take part in after-school activities?
Well I loved just hanging out with my friends, but most of all I loved ballet and went to extra classes after school.

Did you have any pets while you were at school?
My parents weren't animal lovers so we were only allowed a goldfish! But since I had my two daughters, we've had loads – two cats, two guinea pigs, two rabbits, two hamsters and two goldfish.

What was your most embarrassing moment?
When I was eleven I had to play piano for assembly. It was April Fool's Day and the piano wouldn't work (it turned out that someone had put a book in the back). I couldn't bring myself to stand up and investigate because that would draw attention to me, so I sat there with my hands on the keys wishing to die, until a teacher came and rescued me!

To find out more about Ann Bryant visit her website: www.annbryant.co.uk